Bequeath Them

No Tumbled House

Bequeath Them
No Tumbled House

✴❖✴❖✴❖✴❖✴❖✴

YVONNE MacMANUS

DOUBLEDAY & COMPANY, INC.

GARDEN CITY, NEW YORK, 1977

All of the characters in this book
are fictitious, and any resemblance
to actual persons, living or dead,
is purely coincidental.

Library of Congress Cataloging in Publication Data

MacManus, Yvonne.
Bequeath them no tumbled house.

I. Title.
PZ4.M16595Be [PS3563.A31885]   813'.5'4
ISBN: 0-385-12034-6
Library of Congress Catalog Card Number: 76-16254

Dedication

*Con agradecimiento y cariño
a mi tia, Julia Piña, que nunca
perdio la fe en mi, ni en la vida misma.*

Keep the young generations in hail,
And bequeath them no tumbled house!

—George Meredith,
The Empty Purse

Bequeath Them

No Tumbled House

CHAPTER ONE

When I had last seen the apartment, my mother was still alive, and, as usual, complaining bitterly about living in such a rundown neighborhood—"a ghetto tenement," she called it. I had long ago ceased to argue with her, or to suggest that she move elsewhere if it annoyed her so; Mother was a strong-willed woman, descended from pioneering stock, and getting her even to consider a minor change in her life often seemed to require an act of Congress. Moving an ashtray from one side of the couch to the coffee table was to bring on a tight-lipped grunt of disapproval.

Perhaps I should explain that my mother was chronologically old enough to be my grandmother; she was forty-seven when she gave birth to me. Widowed at forty-one, she already had three children from her first marriage: Alexander, who was twenty-two at the time; Melanie, who was twenty; and William, the baby, who was only seventeen. After two and a half years of widowhood, supported primarily by her husband's small pension fund, and shares in a nearly defunct mine in California, Mother met and married Mr. Horatio G. Laird.

Her contention, she often explained to me, was that she was lonely, and that she felt William still needed the guiding hand of a responsible male adult. If in a good mood while telling me about the "old days," she would laugh, pat my arm, and say that no one was more surprised by her late pregnancy than she had been; if in a bad mood, her voice would trail off as if her greatest burden in life had been my birth. These reminis-

cences would almost always take place after one of her simple, rib-sticking dinners, while still seated at the round oak
dining table—which always bore her only lace tablecloth—
aged to a mottled yellow and showing puckers of too many
inept mendings—over an oilcloth to protect the table surface.
As was common in the days when these old apartment buildings went up in Boston, the dining room was a comfortable
size, with hardwood floors and high ceilings. The walls were
papered in a pattern no longer to be discerned, and Mother's
few framed pictures were hung by brownish red silk cords
from the molding about eighteen inches from the ceiling. And
while the apartment had been converted to electricity, the
original wall fixtures remained, with their brass fittings and
frosted globes, which were inadequate to the task of shielding
out the harshness of 100-watt bulbs. It never seemed to occur
to Mother that she didn't have to use such strong bulbs; it was
in character, I suppose, for her to take full advantage of the
facilities—if electricity is available, well, then, let us have light
and lots of it! Lord only knows what an antique dealer would
retail those old fixtures for these days, but as a child, I was always fascinated with them, trying to imagine what the room
would have been like when it was new, filled with distin-
guished guests at a proper dining table. And it seemed to me
that we were the only people in the world whose light
switches consisted of two round buttons in the wall—push one
on top, and the lights went on; push one on the bottom, and
they went off. I rather doubt that Mother ever saw a modern-
day light switch that merely flipped upward or downward, but
even if she had, I'm sure she would have thought it an im-
practical cheap device—despite the fact that we often had
problems with the push buttons jamming in the wall.

However, with such a disparity in our ages, my mother and
I never had an opportunity to relate to each other in a tradi-
tional fashion. By the time I was ten, Mother was already
fifty-seven. Moreover, Mother had spent most of her life on
the West Coast, in a small community that depended upon
mining for its survival; her life had been a series of hardships
until she married Mr. Laird. She would never address herself
directly to the reason we had moved to Boston, and almost
never mentioned her life with Mr. Laird—as she always re-

ferred to him. The transition to an apartment in a crowded city must have been enormous; and as I grew older, I assumed that her unspoken reasons must have been even greater.

Fortunately for me, I had never known any other place to live but Boston; I wasn't even a year old when we moved there. I grew up never knowing my father, or even my half brothers and sister. Stickball on the sidewalk had never struck me as anything resembling a deprived childhood; and nothing could ever be more exciting than a broken water main in August. But Mother was a harsh parent, unyielding, and not given to any display of affection. In a sense, I raised myself; as long as I was never caught in the act of doing something Mother considered wrong, I was left very much to my own amusement. By the time I was in my teens, I began to feel a lack in communication. With a double generation gap, one never asked questions about boys or sex, much less about menstruation. When I was old enough for my first period, I was stunned with unbelieving fear and convinced that I should be rushed to the hospital. Instead, Mother tore up an old muslin sheet, folded it into six neat overlays, and gave me instructions on its use and the importance of cleanliness; she never uttered one word about the bleeding being normal, a sign of my physical maturation . . . and she'd never heard about Kotex, which I later learned about from a gym teacher. If one were to write down every cliché adage known to the English language, my mother not only believed in them all, but she virtually personified them. A penny saved is a penny earned; waste not, want not; and so on and so on. Growing up around my mother was a strong lesson in endurance and survival.

But now she was dead and it was my responsibility to clear her things out of the apartment. A week before, she had suffered a heart attack, lingering on only three days till her death. I'd been summoned at once, of course, so I was able to be with her during her last conscious moments. Illness and death are never pleasant companions, but to watch so indomitable a woman as my mother unable to get her breath, a grayish pallor to her heavily lined face, was a horrible experience. While we were never what anyone could call "close," nonetheless we each had a strong respect for the other and, as much as she would permit me, I loved her.

As I walked listlessly through the empty rooms, memories invaded my mind and brought unwanted tears to my eyes; tears I would not permit to spill over . . . Mother would not have approved. The overstuffed sofa with the once-blue upholstery now a dull gray, the protective linen doilies on each sagging arm, which Mother had paid for on installment, faithfully going down to the store every Friday afternoon, at 3:00 sharp, to count out her coins. I'd been too little to be able to see above the ledge of the payment window, glimpsing only the forehead and bald pate of the man who took her money, dully hearing his "Thank you, Mrs. Laird, see you next Friday," through the thick glass partition, and hearing the whoosh of the chuted container to the cashier's office. If possible, the department store was older than our apartment, and no one had ever bothered to renovate it. The wing-back chair, which Mother had found discarded, sat at a no-nonsense right angle to the sofa; how many nights had she spent up late at the sewing machine making slipcovers? It didn't matter very much now; the fabric was slick with use since it was her favorite chair. Between them, the etched brass floor lamp with its dull onyx base supported on squat, brass lions' paws clutching at the worn carpet, its fluted shade a pasty ivory with sections of the fringe missing like gaps in a denture. Behind it, on the wall, the dime-store framed photo of me when I graduated from high school—all confident smiles, the first-permitted use of lipstick on a young mouth that would have looked better without it, the eyebrows still ignorant of tweezers, the optimistic gray eyes . . . how young I looked, how guileless. The summer of '62; I'd just turned seventeen. My mother had given me my first all-leather handbag—a lady can always be told by her handbag—and my best friend had given me a gold-plated link bracelet with a Pisces charm. My graduation present to her had been a boxed edition of Beethoven's symphonies on stereophonic LPs; lavishly foolish, of course, but I had very few friends and, I suppose, my gratitude for her friendship was out of proportion to reality. At seventeen, I believed that friends remained so until romantic death; at thirty, I knew better.

Mother had at first refused me permission to attend the graduation dance; but relented later and set about to make me a suitable dress, one that I need not "be ashamed of because we're poor!" I had been so elated at her revised decision that I'd cheerfully have danced in a barrel—or so it seemed to me now that it was thirteen years later.

There were no other photos in the living room. In fact, it was a room which strongly reflected my mother's personality: an imitation maple cobbler's bench for a coffee table, a picture of F.D.R. on the far wall, a small mahogany-veneered table on the far end of the sofa with a milk-glass table lamp on it, and the only ashtray in the entire apartment—as a silent concession to my "filthy unladylike habit"; it was doubtlessly the ugliest ashtray ever manufactured, and in all likelihood, Mother had picked it intentionally as a not-so-subtle rebuff.

I stood in the center of the room and let my mind wander. The times I'd stood before her as she strained to read my report card, her metal-framed glasses slipping down her thin nose; the time she'd grabbed me by the hair as I tried to run away from a spanking; the day I'd spilled a chocolate ice-cream cone down the front of my birthday dress and had been afraid to come home—not terribly endearing memories, but they were all I had.

Even on her deathbed, breathlessly and painfully gasping out her last words to me, Mother had remained unemotional. She did, however, find the strength to touch her fingers to mine and say, "You've been a good daughter, Alyce. Not much trouble at all."

"Shh, Mother, save your strength," I replied, a knot forming tightly in my throat. It was as close as she'd ever come to telling me that she loved me. While she characteristically had said that I'd not been much trouble—implying that I had been *some* trouble—nonetheless, I knew what she wanted to say and was unable to without feeling like a sentimental old fool. She was seventy-seven, and not about to change her habits merely because she was dying. The room had reeked of camphor and medications, of old age and the damp presence of death—I have wondered since why there is such a heavy humidity around a deathbed.

But these thoughts were not accomplishing what I'd gone to

the apartment to do. I glanced at her favorite chair, momentarily thought I could see her seated there, and smiled at my overactive imagination. For a split second, I thought I should excuse myself before her empty chair, asking her consent for my withdrawal as I'd always done. Instead, I symbolically ran my hand over the back of it, giving it a few pats of farewell, then went into the kitchen and placed the chipped enamel pot on the gas stove to boil some water for tea. Then I went into her bedroom.

The shades were pulled down, and the recently starched flowered curtains stood stiffly away from the peeling casement as if afraid of contamination. It seemed logical to begin with Mother's closet, and I couldn't prevent the grimace of fond recollection as I opened the heavy door and was overwhelmed with the pungent odor of mothballs. It was, somehow, fitting— as if my mother's entire life had been wrapped in mothballs and the closet were merely an extension of this safeguard. I had a surging feeling of compassion for her which bordered pity, but not quite. What hopes and dreams had she entertained as a girl, what fantasies of romance had occupied her? It was very difficult to envision the sinewy, weathered woman I'd known all my life as a dancing, laughing wisp of a girl at a square dance in some remote western town. See her now, sipping sarsaparilla, my imagination coaxed; or there, do-se-doing with that handsome young miner . . . will he try to kiss her? No, such things simply didn't jell with the woman I had known. Three black cotton dresses, a dull cotton frock, two recently purchased housedresses from J. C. Penney's, a heavy winter cloth coat and a lighter, spring coat, a brown skirt, and three blouses. That was her wardrobe. Two pairs of sturdy walking shoes, black of course, and a rarely worn pair of patent-leather shoes with boulevard heels. Granted, she had been buried in her best dress and best shoes—a dull rose woolen dress—yet the closet was barren despite being so small it wouldn't have held even half my own wardrobe. It was the closet of someone who goes nowhere, and never entertains company; it was the closet of someone who lived through each day very much as the day before, year in and year out.

I gritted my teeth and placed things neatly on her bed, pulling down her one suitcase as a practical way of getting her few modest things to the Goodwill. There were several old shoe boxes on the shelf, which contained such valuables as my birth certificate, my smallpox and polio vaccination papers, her first wedding certificate, and a few old letters with three-cent postage and "Buy War Bonds" stamped across them. Those I put in my handbag to examine at some later time, when the awful sense of loss was past. At last, the closet was empty, and I turned my attention to her chiffonier.

Most of the drawers were less than half full; the usual things—underwear of the cotton variety, lisle stockings rolled into neat muffs, a pair of summer and a pair of winter gloves, a box of heavy hairpins, her comb and brush . . . that sort of thing. But the bottom drawer was a surprise.

It contained old photographs. Loose and jumbled, as if she'd thrown them in there to be rid of them yet not having the heart to literally throw them away. All of them were from before I was born, except a few that showed a strikingly handsome middle-aged woman holding an infant in her arms; I assumed I was the baby, and the woman had to be my mother. I'd never known she had any photographs at all, much less this cluttered assortment from her past, some bent or torn, and many of them sepia prints.

I ran to the kitchen to get a shopping bag, realized I'd forgotten about the boiling water for tea, and then returned to the bedroom to place them all in the bag as carefully as I could. Like a child searching for fallen coins at the seashore, a sense of elation and delighted anticipation filled my thoughts. Perhaps I'd be able to reconstruct my mother's life through them, see her world as the man beneath the black hood captured the moment through his upside-down viewing lens. At least, they would give me *some*thing to go on. Did she smile a great deal before I was born? Was there, perhaps, a picture of my father? And my half brothers? An antiquarian unearthing a first edition could not have been more excited than I as I lifted them from the drawer to the shopping bag. There had to be hundreds of snapshots, which I knew had been taken with a more modern camera, which for so spartan a woman was startling enough. However, I was totally unprepared for the thick envelope beneath them all. It was a manilla envelope, and sealed. On the face of it was written, in my mother's firm schoolgirl penmanship: "Miss Alyce Prather Laird, *For her eyes alone in the event of my death.*"

How like her to have used her own family surname as if there were more than one Alyce Laird in Boston. I turned it over in my hands, half expecting invisible ink to appear on its surface, and wondered if perhaps she had left me instructions for how prudently to spend the balance of my life. Or perhaps, perhaps she had expressed to me, after death, those motherly sentiments she could never bring herself to say in life.

I rose from my kneeling position and took the envelope with me to the kitchen, placing it carefully on the linoleum-covered table while I made myself the long delayed cup of tea, glancing at the envelope from time to time, speculating on what it could possibly contain.

While the tea steeped, I sat down on the wooden chair before the envelope. Even though the envelope had my name clearly written on its face, I somehow felt like I was invading my mother's privacy, like a sneak who should steam open the seal to avoid detection later. What on earth would she write down that she couldn't have told me before her death? Was I —ridiculous as I knew the thought to be—illegitimate? Was there insanity in the Prather family?

It was so totally unlike her to have done something like that; to write a communique when we lived in the same city and I visited her at least once a week. But then, I reasoned, so was a drawerful of old photographs, which she'd never mentioned to me, much less shown to me. Yes, of course, she had been taciturn about her life with her second husband; even secretive, if one is given to drama. However, Mother had carefully instilled within me a deep respect for the privacy of others. How often had she reminded me, "If I want you to know about it, I'll tell you. It's downright rude to ask personal questions of others!" It hadn't taken too long for me to learn that I'd find out more if I didn't ask than if I did—except about her life with Horatio G. Laird. She volunteered almost nothing about my father, and I eventually gave up asking.

Perhaps that was the contents of the envelope . . . ?

As if my mother were watching, I forced myself to pour a cup of tea before opening the envelope—it would have been unseemly in her eyes to rip it open, as I was strongly tempted to do. But having shown my restraint to my own satisfaction, I proceeded to tear the top of it slowly and neatly, and extract the eight-by-ten white paper it contained. "Daughter, Alyce," it began.

There was no reason to tell you before now. If you'd gotten married, as I hoped you would, there'd be no reason to tell you at all. A good man would have provided for you. Since you have not seen fit to marry, you may want to take advantage of the information I'm about to give you. That's up to you. I wouldn't recommend it, but it's your right to make up your own mind.

Your father, Horatio G. Laird, was murdered in the prime of his life. I never knew the who or the why of it, and in my grief, I did not pursue the matter. Moreover, shortly following his untimely death, there were threats made against my life and yours as well—infant though you still were. They were never honest, out in the open warnings, but printed messages wrapped around rocks and thrown through the windows, or messages left under the door. They were never signed.

Because there had been some arguing between your father and his two business partners, having to do with the mine, I have assumed that one or both of the partners killed your father, and drove me away with my child. Since no threats were ever directed against the children of my first marriage, it seems logical that the culprit had to be one of the partners, and you, as legal heir to the Laird share of the mine, posed, I presume, an equal obstacle to their plans for the mine. While I might well have stood my ground and fought for my rights—as well as bring the murderer to justice—I didn't dare risk your life. You were too young to have any say in my decision, but I'd brought you into the world, and it was my responsibility to keep you healthy and alive for as long as God's will would permit it.

I don't know what's happened to the mine or your father's interests financially. My guess is that the estate is worth millions, if the lode didn't peter out. For quite some time, I remained in touch only with our family friend and lawyer, Mansfield Watersdown. His offices were in Los Angeles, but he had a cabin up near us. If you want to claim your birthright, look him up. He'd be pretty old by now, or he may even be dead. But if he's still alive, he would be the best one to advise you on how to proceed.

As you know, we have not exactly had a luxurious life, you and me. But we always managed to lead clean, decent, and God-fearing lives. I trust this letter will not change you in that regard. And the only reason I'm telling you about all this is because both the partners are dead now, and could no longer be a threat to you.

You might also want to contact your half brothers and sister. Because I feared so for your life, I have had no contact with them lest we be traced by way of correspondence or telephone calls. As you'll recall, their surname, my first husband's, is Musser. If you need help, see if you can find them.

If you decide to go to California, I wish you success in locating and claiming your fortune. If you'll always remember that God is with you, you cannot go too far wrong.

Your devoted mother,

Juliana Prather Laird

Fortune? Skulduggery? California mining towns and murder? It was more than I could quite assimilate at one sitting. I stared at her terse bequest, which gave and took away at one and the same time, with incredulity. But one thing was absolutely certain: The threats must have been frighteningly convincing to force my mother to move away, and live in poverty all those years, when she had a legal right to a fortune. And my mother did not frighten easily!

CHAPTER TWO

For the next few days I seemed in two worlds. One, of course, my usual life, which consisted of going to work Monday through Friday as the administrative assistant director of the Language Arts Department, Boston Christian College. The best thing about the job was its location to my small apartment; I could walk to work even in the most inclement weather. And too, probably because of the shortage of money during my childhood, the security of the job meant a good deal to me; short of embezzlement, or running off for an illicit weekend with the college president, the academic world is loath to fire its nonacademic employees. While I've met a few people who lead more exciting lives than I do, most of the time it seems to me that the crux of it lies in the very insecurity of their lives. It may sound terribly pedantic and dull, but I'm afraid that my psyche would shatter without health insurance and retirement plans. At least, so I had always thought—up until finding that letter from my mother.

Suddenly, as if a part of me had been in a coma for the past thirty years, I found myself sorting through Mother's old photographs with all the absorption of a miner panning for gold. The full-length skirts, the middy blouses, knickers, and narrow lapels ending at the top button of the jacket . . . it wasn't too difficult to figure out which one was Alexander, or William, or Melanie—my mother's first family—once I was able to determine that it was truly she in many of the pictures. An angular face, but not sternly so, I was surprised to see how much I resembled my mother. The same thick dark brown hair—or so it seemed in the sepia photos—and the large gray eyes topped by uninteresting straight-line eyebrows; a rather full mouth, perhaps a little too wide for the approval of fashion, especially in those days when petite cupid-bow lips were more desirable. The nose was long but well-shaped, the cheekbones high, the brow wide with an uneven hairline, and the jaw hinting at a strong stubborn streak.

It was incredible, like looking at myself in a costume movie. The woman I had known bore no resemblance to the woman in the photos. In fact, on more than one occasion during my youth, I had contemplated the possibility that I was an adopted child; not only because of Mother's age, but because I could see no resemblance between us. My mother, as I knew her, was stooped and gnarled, her hair gray and listless; the face, lined from too much time in the sun, was almost leathery in appearance, and the expression she always wore was one of tolerant retreat from the world. Now, of course, I knew why; it could not have been easy for her to give up her legal fortune and flee with her child lest harm befall them both. And while I'd often heard others say how our inner selves, our thoughts, mold our faces, I'd not realized before how it had disguised my mother from me. The woman I knew was hard, bitter, severe, and unflappable. The woman in these old photos was outgoing, warm, smiling, proud of her family; it was very difficult to believe it was the same person. But at least there could be no lingering doubts about my adoption; I was nearly a dead-ringer for my mother when she was much younger.

And little by little, a nagging anger began to grow within me. A sense of outrage, not so much for me, but for what those associates of my father had done to us both—my mother, more than me, because she had to live with the knowledge all those years. While I could not conceive of this instance as illustration that ignorance is bliss, nonetheless I never had to face any sense of loss or injustice . . . until recently. I silently thanked my mother for her good judgment. Had she told me from childhood about this fortune awaiting me, no doubt I would have grown up filled with hate and resentment toward our enforced poverty. The information would doubtlessly have tainted my every waking moment, and I was glad that

my mother's shrewd pioneer stock had given her the good
sense to realize it and spare me such a burden.

Yet, during those few days, my anger mounted and I felt
nearly compelled to seek justice—even after so many years. If
a fortune did indeed await me, I could have Mother exhumed
and moved to a nicer cemetery, and give her a proper tombstone—such things mattered to her, as I suppose they do to
most people of her generation. How often I'd heard her wistfully say, "I'd like to go to my final rest where there's a lot of
trees, a place with cool shade and fine big lawns." On other
occasions, she'd say, "Wouldn't it be just fine, Alyce, if I could
be laid to rest with a big guardian angel watching over me? A
fine statue that would tell others that here lies a God-fearing
woman! Yes, yes, I surely would like a big angel standing over
me for all eternity!"

Instead, she was buried in the open sun; and in a vertical
position because the old cemetery was too crowded for hori-
zontal burial. A stone marked her grave; a very, very small
stone with barely enough room to have inscribed: JULIANA
LAIRD 1898–1975. I'd wanted to add both her maiden name
and her first married name, but there simply was no place to
write it. Staring at the facsimile of that younger Juliana, how I
seethed with resentment at her fate. How was it possible that
in 1945 crime went unpunished? How could they have murdered my father, and threatened my mother, and not have
been brought to trial? It wasn't as if it were during the settling of the Old West, with everyone taking the law into his
own hands. Although I'd never been out of Boston—except for
brief excursions to Martha's Vineyard or New York City—
nonetheless I found it nearly impossible to believe that California was still a lawless land in '45! Perhaps my mother had
not fully understood the facts, or had misconstrued state-
ments. The whole thing simply seemed preposterous, yet—

Well, I had a choice. Either I could continue my life and
forget about "foul play" and "amassed fortunes awaiting," or
I could go to California and find out for myself precisely what
the truth was. If I remained in Boston—washing my hair on
Monday nights, going to the college recreation center on
Wednesdays to play bridge with other single misfits, doing my
laundry and ironing on Thursdays—I would never know the

truth, and I would certainly never improve my financial status. Since graduating from college, my life had been pretty much the same, month in and month out. And I suddenly realized that I was doing the same thing my mother had done: just existing from one day to the next. How often had I paused to calculate my exact age, unsure if I were twenty-nine or thirty-one . . . merely because there were no highlights or lows in my life, no events to mark off the years. With indignant chagrin, I realized that there was more than just a physical resemblance to my mother; I was also following in her footsteps with my life. I too lived in a cocoon, afraid the world might harm me, the routine of my life serving as dunnage.

I picked up the one photo I planned to have restored and framed, and stared at my mother's image as she tenderly held me in her arms. "Mother," I whispered at her, "I'm going to get you an angel . . . or join you trying!"

✳✧✳

"I don't know whether to have you committed or send up flares of congratulation," Tharon Ann said, her eyes craftily gauging the marital status of two businessmen who sat opposite us at the airport bar. Tharon Ann Ward was my closest friend; or more accurately, I was hers—she knew practically nothing about me, but I knew every detail of her entire life. Tharon Ann liked to talk and, finding good listeners scarce, she had befriended me five years before while we both worked in the Language Arts Department. She'd left three years ago to get married, and have a baby—in that order—but we'd somehow remained friends despite lack of common interests.

"Tharon," I whispered, "you can stop looking at those two men . . . you're not only married, but a mother."

She brought her glance back to me and smiled innocently. "Why Alyce Laird! That doesn't mean I'm *dead!* You should just see the way Harry ogles the ladies whenever we're out somewhere—it's positively shameful!"

One of the men must've overheard her; his face broke into a grin and he inclined his head toward me the way royalty nods to the lines of people who watch them ride by. While I didn't blush, I was terribly embarrassed. "Anyway," I said after a momentary silence, "my going to California isn't like Marco Polo off in search of the route to India. It isn't as if I'd quit my job, Tharon. I'm on an open-ended leave, which means I can come back whenever I want to."

"Yes, I guess so, Alyce, but you've absolutely no friends out there . . . no one to look up who'd be interested in your welfare. I mean, I know that California isn't Rangoon, but it *is* a long way from here and you've never, well, what I mean is . . ."

I had to laugh as she fumbled for the right thing to say. "What you mean is that you don't think I'm capable of taking care of myself?"

"Well, you have led a very sheltered life, Alyce. It isn't as if you were a world traveler, or accustomed to being in strange places all by yourself." She toyed with the ice in her old-fashioned, glancing furtively about before sneaking a cube to her mouth.

"I've had my own apartment for five years, Tharon Ann. And I've been totally self-supporting. You made the same remarks when I went to New York on my vacation two years ago, remember? And I managed to survive that big, bad city all on my own."

"Umm, maybe. But having your own apartment isn't the same as being independent. You've always relied on your mother for so much, Alyce, though why I'll never know . . . she never said a kind word to you that I can recall."

"I loved my mother, that's all the reason anyone needs. And anyone who dared to smoke in front of her had to have the courage of the Christian martyrs!"

"Well, I can see that you're bound and determined to go out there. . . ."

I watched a huge plane, a 747 I think, roll past us and was grateful for the thick glass that kept out most of the noise. "Besides," I added, "I do have people to look up. My mother's children from her first marriage. We are related, after all."

"Some family!" she snorted with a wave of her petite plump hand. "Children who never even bothered to keep in touch with their own mother!"

"They did try," I explained to Tharon Ann for the umpteenth time. "Those letters from my father's lawyer, Mansfield

Watersdown, told us that." I could envision the neat hand-writing of those old letters, the ample space between the script: *Your children continue to ask for you, Juliana. They refuse to believe that I don't know where you are. What should I tell them?* Yes, she was sure that she would find a sense of family among Alexander, William, and Melanie; they too were her mother's children, and once they knew why their mother had dropped out of sight, they would help me to unearth the truth about my father's death, and what happened to the estate. I was sure of it.

". . . If only you had written to them saying you were coming out, I'd feel a lot better," Tharon prattled on, never realizing that I had tuned out temporarily.

"Where would I have written to?" I asked with a slight smile. "The last known address was someplace called Frazier, and that was in 1945. Who knows where any of them are now?"

"Or even if they're still alive," Tharon added with growing alarm.

I glanced at my watch for the fifteenth time in the past fifteen minutes, terribly conscious that flight announcements couldn't be heard in the lounge. Actually I needn't have bothered to worry about missing my flight; I knew perfectly well that the man who was alone at the bar had been ahead of me at the check-in counter, and all I had to do was keep an eye on him.

". . . What would you do then?"

"W-what?" I asked apologetically. I hadn't heard a word Tharon had said in the past few moments, and I was naturally embarrassed to be so remiss.

"If none of your family is still alive, what then?"

"There's no reason to think they wouldn't be," I said slowly, not really wishing to contemplate such a possibility. "They'd only be in their fifties. Besides, they're bound to have children of their own by now. And too, there's still Mr. Watersdown—though there's a better chance that he may not still be alive."

Tharon giggled. "I *adore* that name! Wouldn't it be just too funny for a bartender to have that name?"

"But then," I continued, ignoring her aside, "there's got to be a hall of records somewhere. Title deeds alone would probably tell me the last known address in case my father's lands were sold to someone else."

Tharon inhaled deeply, thrusting her empty drink away from her. "Well, it all sounds like a wild-goose chase to me. Has it occurred to you that maybe your mother was a little dingy in the head? That maybe she'd just imagined all that stuff about murders and threats and vast fortunes?"

I laughed. "You met Mother. Do you think she was dingy?"

"No," Tharon conceded. "I suppose not. No one who was as sure of herself as your mother was could possibly freak out."

We sat in silence for a few moments, watching the planes taxi in and taxi out, sometimes seeing them whiz by at a more distant runway. I had only been on an airplane once before in my life, and that was for the return trip from New York City. I had gone there by train, enjoying the chance to see the countryside and small towns, but after ten days in that mad city, I couldn't wait to get back home to Boston. I only hoped that Los Angeles wasn't like New York; if one went by movies and TV, there didn't seem to be any similarity at all. But then, the few times I'd seen a movie set in Boston, I had to admit it was a highly distorted view of my hometown. Things either looked much seedier, or infinitely more handsome; and everything seemed larger than it really was. And, of course, I had absolutely no idea where this Frazier place was—it could've been a nice city or a ghost town, for all I knew.

At a nearby table, five young people sat down, all talking at once and obviously filled with fun and excitement. One young man was carrying a covered tennis racquet, and a sweet-faced young girl held a Samsonite make-up case on her lap. They looked young enough to be a honeymoon couple being sent off by friends, but they seemed much too self-assured for the fantasy to fit properly. More assured, I thought, than I am. And for the first time, I began to feel excitement about this adventure—my first and only adventure, I acknowledged ruefully, in my entire life! I was now a totally free person. I didn't have to think twice before every decision to outguess what my mother would think about it, nor did I have to answer her terse questions about my activities. Oh, I realized years ago that I never really had to report back to her, that I could have told her it was none of her business; but I couldn't. As far as I knew then, I was her only kin—in Boston, anyway—and I knew that her questions were not really so much a probing into my private affairs as they were a vicarious sharing with me. All my mother had in the world, as far as I knew, was me; if I had to rearrange things a little to accommodate her wishes, it wasn't such a terrible hardship.

Certainly, I had asserted myself from time to time, found areas in which to rebel—such as my smoking, or going to New York alone—but for the most part, I consciously tried not to cause her any worry . . . or shame. Even when I had been so infatuated with a senior in college, who'd asked me to marry him, my mother's wishes were terribly important to me. I'd brought him home—isn't that strange, but I seem to have forgotten his name . . . it was Fred, I think. He'd not liked her, and had been unable to conceal it. That was it; that put the lid on any interest I'd had in him. There was just my mother and me, and if you wanted me, you at least had to be civil to my mother. I never expected anyone to adore her, merely to get along with her and show the proper respect. That never seemed to me to be asking so much. And after Fred, I dated several other young men from time to time; but I could never take them very seriously. Some of them were interested only in sex and, as you might imagine, my upbringing would not permit me so loose an approach for social approval. A couple of them spoke round-aboutly about marriage, but it was easy to see that what they really meant was a housekeeper who'd bear them children. And little by little, I'd begun to withdraw from the mating race. Somewhere along the line, somehow, I'd subconsciously decided that I was not good marriage material—perhaps one could say that I became an old maid by the time I was twenty-six or -seven. The games and lies, the little coy glances or covert overtures; they all seemed very adolescent to me. But then, I wondered, perhaps it was because my mother had been so much older than I; perhaps I was old before my time.

Thinking about it that winter evening in the airport lounge, it occurred to me that I'd never really had a childhood, the way others do. Thriftiness, cleanliness, integrity, and all those other noble qualities had been placed upon my shoulders even before I could really remember. Laughter had not been a part of my upbringing, nor song nor dance, nor the warm affection of loving relatives come to visit—perhaps with a surprise present, or a new riddle. The closest thing I had to a relative was Franklin Delano Roosevelt's portrait hanging on the living-room wall; and even that was just a cheap print, slightly off-register.

No wonder my elation was seeping through the locks of my mind's canals; for thirty years I had lived trapped within myself, my emotions clamped tightly shut against the dreaded hurt that caring was bound to incur. Well, even iron erodes in time, and now my time had come. I was free, I was going far away, and—I smiled to myself as I saw the fresh snow begin to fall on the runway, knowing that I'd soon be in sunny Los Angeles—perhaps I would find adventure . . . and romance. I would have to buy some new clothes, something colorful and carefree to bolster my courage for this new role. After all, I had three thousand dollars in a savings account—squirreled away every paycheck with ten dollars here, fifty there—and if I didn't want my life to end at thirty, it was going to take some radical re-evaluation of myself.

". . . We'll sure miss you at Christmas, Alyce," Tharon Ann was saying.

"I'll send you a card," I replied inanely.

"How will I know where to write to you?"

I spotted the fellow at the bar glance at his watch, wave to the bartender as he pulled out his wallet, and I looked at my own watch yet again. It was only twenty minutes before flight time. My pulse began to race as I waved to our waitress for the check, trying to make sensible answers to Tharon's countless last-minute questions as I gathered up my hand valise and purse, fumbling to have my ticket at the ready.

Tharon raced alongside me as we ran for the boarding gate, and at the last second, she threw her arms around my neck and kissed my cheek. Noises invaded my brain. People everywhere saying their good-byes, the sharp escalating whistles of jets coming and going, blaring announcements over loudspeakers. It was a cacophonous choral of a world in transit, coming or going, but loud in either direction. I had no idea of what would happen to me in the next few weeks, or even months, but whatever it was, it had to be better than the first thirty years of my life.

I gave Tharon Ann a swift hug in return, promising I'd write as soon as I had an address, and fled down the carpeted hallway before she could cry—or I would.

CHAPTER THREE

We arrived in Los Angeles at 10 P.M., their time. I've never understood why there are time zones; it seemed bizarre that the plane could have left Boston at 7 P.M., be in the air for six hours—which puts one into the next day, technically—and yet arrive somewhere else on the day one left. There's something wrong about it, as if the Mad Hatter ran the airlines, or Dali. For people like me, I suppose it's just as well that the supersonic jets are not in operation; as I understand it, you'd arrive somewhere before you'd even left your embarkation point. Frightening.

But my confused senses were not foremost on my list of importance. Like any gawking tourist, my attention was devoted to new sights, impressions, and, because it was one in the morning to my system, on staying awake.

What struck me at once was the absence of tall buildings. I suppose, if one were to be completely objective, it wasn't very different in suburban Boston, but somehow I'd expected something more spectacular from Los Angeles; after all, it was the home of Hollywood, Beverly Hills, glamour and make-believe. It seemed, on the drive to my hotel, that everything was made of stucco, rarely above one story, and that there was an incredible overuse of neon lights. Moreover, everywhere I looked, there were massive billboards.

I didn't know enough about the town to know how many routes there were to Hollywood, but there seemed to be very little traffic. We drove past what seemed to be low-income housing developments, and then into hills where huge bobbing structures dotted the terrain. Leaning forward, I asked the cabbie what they were.

"Oil derricks," he replied. "First time in L.A.?"

"Yes, it is."

He snorted. "You'll see oil derricks just about anywhere in this town. You'll get used to them."

I sat back in the seat and marveled at the strangeness of this community; but then, I reasoned, Los Angeles had probably been a boom town in its own way, and the discovery of oil-rich acreage would certainly have influenced how the city grew, how it was built. And one could certainly see the influence of the automobile; the streets and highways were beautifully paved and kept in perfect repair, street signs were clearly readable, and as we drew closer to the city itself, large, illuminated signs proclaimed the name of the upcoming intersection. All very practical, and all obviously for the convenience of motorists.

We sped up a nearly deserted commercial street called La Brea. While my job at the Language Arts Department didn't require that I speak any languages, it didn't take too much to figure out that it was a Spanish name, which I also assumed with such street names as La Tijera, La Cienega. It made everything seem a little more exotic, and I was glad they had kept the original flavor of the city—by street names, if nothing else. And, of course, I was also captivated with how many trees there were, though most of them looked like one-hundred-foot telephone poles wearing Carmen Miranda hats; these, I soon learned, were typical California non-fruit-bearing palm trees . . . and they were everywhere.

In moments, the cab pulled up in front of the Hollywood Roosevelt Hotel. I'd chosen it because the travel agency had said it was centrally located, not one of those sterile modern hotels, and quite simply, because it appealed to me to be staying in the heart of Hollywood, directly across the street from the famous Grauman's Chinese Theatre . . . except now it was called Mann's Chinese. The fare on the meter read $7.80, so I gave the driver a ten. The doorman carried my luggage to the reception desk, and shortly after, I was taken to my room. It was on the south side of the hotel, on the sixth floor, and commanded a view of Los Angeles that was nearly breath-taking. For as far as the eye could see, lights twinkled across flat areas and up over hills; traffic was sparse, but the neon signs shone colorfully. And from the windows, I could see that there were areas of Los Angeles with high-rises after all. The famous freeways were clearly visible, and automobile lights moved like drops of bright red and white mercury—and, naturally, palm trees shattered the city skyline like surrealistic sentries.

It was beautiful, but I was exhausted. I felt as if I'd slept in the same clothes for ten days, and I won't begin to describe what my teeth felt like to my tongue; and I was relatively confident that I could light my cigarettes with my own breath. Too exhausted even for a bath, I crawled into the double bed, eternally grateful for the invention of the mattress, and fell into a dead sleep almost at once. The unfamiliar bed, strange hotel noises, and the different tempo of street sounds aroused my consciousness from time to time, but not enough for me to consider myself awake.

The next day was Tuesday, and I had already left a seven o'clock wake-up call. I intended to get as good a night's rest as I could before the task of tracking down Mansfield Watersdown, attorney-at-law.

✳◌✳

A swift check of the Yellow Pages the next morning showed no attorneys by the name of Watersdown. But after three cups of black coffee and a poached egg on toast in the coffee shop downstairs, I inquired at the information desk how I might go about checking for him. The clerk pointed me to their telephone switchboard office, and in front of it were all the directories for the Greater Los Angeles area—eight of them! Obviously, each major section of town had its own directory; there was Beverly Hills, Long Beach, San Fernando Valley, on and on. It boggled the mind to think of one single city requiring so many telephone books, but there they were. And I'd have gone through all of them if a kindly operator hadn't explained to me that the directories covered the entire 213 dialing area, but that certain sections were not considered part of L.A. by the "natives." The only lawyer by that name either of us could find was in an area known as Northridge, out in the San Fernando Valley: Watersdown, Langdon, and Shapiro, 113758 Balboa Blvd., Northridge . . . 887-1101.

"It's an awfully long way, miss, and it would be a toll charge," the operator explained apologetically.

"But it *is* Los Angeles," I verified.

She nodded. "I guess so. I don't know very much about the Valley."

Something in her tone brought images of covered wagons and Indian uprisings. Had she arched her arm slowly, grunting out "Many moons to reach the Valley," I'd not have been surprised. But I didn't see what choice I had; it was the only listing I could find, so I told her to go ahead and place the call for me while I took a booth in the lobby.

"Watersdown, Langdon, and Shapiro, good morning," a girl's voice answered.

"Yes, I wonder if you could help me," I began falteringly, "I'm looking for a lawyer named Mansfield Watersdown, and . . ."

"Mr. Watersdown? One moment, please," she said, but I wasn't at all sure she understood the nature of my question, or even if she'd heard the first name of this particular Watersdown.

Soon another female voice came on the line. "Mr. Watersdown's office, may I help you?"

"Yes, I hope so. I'm looking for a particular Mr. Watersdown . . . I'm not even sure if your employer is the right one. . . ."

"Yes?"

"Uh, Mr. Mansfield Watersdown . . . he would be quite elderly, perhaps retired."

There was a short pause on her end. "Well, our Mr. Watersdown's first name is Eric. I don't recall any Mansfield."

"Perhaps," I interjected, "perhaps it would be his father? Or an uncle, perhaps? There aren't any other lawyers by that name in all of Los Angeles, surely the coincidence is too great."

"Mansfield, you say?" she repeated.

"Yes, that's right."

"Well, I've been with our Mr. Watersdown for six years, but hold on a second, will you? I'll ask him directly."

"Thanks, miss, thank you very much," I said and slumped back against the cold metal of the booth. I hadn't realized how nervous I was until that moment; my hands felt damp and it seemed unbearably hot in the small booth while I waited for the faceless secretary to come back on the line. It was silly of me to feel so nervous just over a telephoned inquiry. On the other hand, I reassured myself, it was an awkward situation; I was a stranger in a new town, trying to find another stranger. Perhaps if I'd been tracking down some old friend, someone who would answer with "Alyce! How wonderful to hear from you!" it might have been different. As it was, I felt like the wrong end of the horse.

"Hello?" asked the secretary's voice, verifying that the line hadn't gone dead.

"Yes, I'm still here," I answered, sitting upright again, as if waiting to hear my name called so I could go up to receive my diploma.

"I'm sorry, miss, but Mr. Watersdown has never heard of anyone by the name of Mansfield. Perhaps the party you're seeking is named Waterton or Waterford . . . we get quite a few erroneous calls for those names."

"No, I'm afraid not. It's the same as your employer's. Well," I sighed, "thank you anyway. You've been most kind."

"I really am sorry," she reiterated. "If he's that elderly, though, perhaps he's retired. Why don't you try some of the retirement communities around Los Angeles? Leisure World, for instance, they have a lot of former professional people over there."

I was too disappointed to ask where it was, and after again thanking the woman, I hung up. Well, that shot my only direct lead. I wondered if the American Bar Association kept a record of former lawyers; it couldn't hurt to try.

The sudden ringing of the telephone jarred me and I automatically picked up the receiver. "Hello," I said, hoping that it wasn't some nut making obscene phone calls to public telephones.

"Miss Laird? It's me, Mona, the switchboard operator."

I smiled with relief. "Hi, Mona."

"Did you get your party all right?"

"No, it was a false lead."

"Now what'll you do?" Mona sounded very involved and concerned, which touched me immediately. "I'm not sure. How about the American Bar Association?"

"We'll give it a try. Stay right there, I'll get the number for you and ring you back."

I replaced the receiver and marveled at what an absolutely charming young girl this Mona was; if everyone in California was that nice, that helpful, it shouldn't be any trouble at all to find Mr. Watersdown or my half brothers and sister! And it occurred to me that just about everyone I had seen since arriving seemed to smile a good deal, certainly more than they smiled in Boston. But then, I reminded myself, I'd not left the hotel lobby yet.

Mona rang me back and said there was no listing for the Bar Association in Los Angeles; the closest she could find was the Committee of Bar Examiners State Bar of California. She placed the call for me and the operator cut in with a new listing for them; we tried again, and this time got through. A young man answered and told me that they wouldn't have any such records, but had I tried the State Bar itself. No. He gave me the telephone number, and Mona got it for me. I explained my problem to the girl who answered, and she transferred me to "records." There I was told that, yes, they did keep a record of all lawyers in the state, even retired ones, but that she couldn't give me that information over the phone; I'd have to come down in person and ask for it.

I opened the booth door and drew in a breath of fresh air, then walked back to Mona's cubicle. "This is the address," I said, waving at her the scrawl I'd made on the inside of a matchbook. "Is it very far?"

"West Third Street? No, not too terribly."

"Could I walk there?"

Mona giggled. "There's nowhere you can walk in Los Angeles, Miss Laird. You'd better plan to rent a car if you'll be doing any running around at all."

"Well, what about a taxi," I countersuggested. I could think of nothing more spendthrift than renting a car when I had no idea of where anything was.

The young girl rolled her eyes upward. "You'll be bankrupt in three days, Miss Laird! Believe me, a car's the only way to get around this town. You can get a taxi out front of a hotel easy enough, but you're never going to find one just meandering up the streets!"

I thanked Mona for her interest, and told her I'd think about it, but for right now, a taxi seemed the most expedient approach. She shook her head like a mother who knows her child must learn his lessons the hard way, but wished me luck.

The ride to Third Street reaffirmed my initial impressions of the city; it was a town which grew outward, not upward. What tall buildings there were obviously had been constructed only recently. Since it was such a lovely view from higher up, I wondered why it had taken so long for Angelenos to take advantage of it. And what struck me as odd was how the main streets were commercial, with shops or movies or whatever, but down almost any side street, it was totally residential; even stranger, a main street might be filled with shops for a number of long, long blocks, and then suddenly become a residential street; or even a large section of town, though bordered by stores, sat squarely and unyieldingly residential. However, while Highland Avenue in Hollywood proper seemed jammed with recording studios, film laboratories, and sound studios, it became a charming, and obviously wealthy, residential section, the street itself divided with old fir and palm trees.

When the taxi arrived at the building that housed the State Bar, I told the cabbie to wait for me, mindful of Mona's forewarning.

"Cost you seven dollars and twenty cents an hour, lady. Sure you want me to wait?"

True daughter of my mother, I gulped at the cost even though I was hopeful it wouldn't take anywhere near so long to get the information I required. "Well, would I be able to find a taxi once you leave?"

He grimaced and scratched his head. "No, probably not, unless you called for one . . . and that could take fifteen, maybe twenty minutes for one to get here."

I began to realize the validity of Mona's advice, but I asked him to wait; this once wouldn't bankrupt me. Fortunately, it took only about ten minutes for me to locate Mansfield Watersdown's last address. Coincidentally, or perhaps not, he had moved to where my half brothers and sister had lived. I wrote it down in my spiral notebook, thanked the clerk, and ran out to the waiting taxi, realizing with a grumbling stomach that it had to be nearly lunchtime. The entire morning had been spent just trying to locate one person; and even with the address I now possessed, I had no way of knowing if he still lived there . . . or even if he was still alive.

Nonetheless, I felt as if I'd really accomplished a good deal, and couldn't resist mentally comparing myself to an over-the-hill Nancy Drew in quest of the "mysterious Mr. Watersdown." But first, I reminded myself, I'd have to find Frazier.

CHAPTER FOUR

After a quick lunch, I obtained a map of California and establishing that Frazier was only a few hours' drive—if that much, I proceeded to rent a car. With steeled nerves, I wheeled out onto Hollywood Boulevard and headed for the Hollywood Freeway, as directed by the rental agency. To my relief, I soon found out that drivers in California take their cars very seriously; they stay in their lanes at a relatively constant speed, and pedestrians are sacrosanct. Although I'd rarely had occasion to drive a car in Boston, I did possess a license; one of my few luxuries in the East was to rent a car in the spring and in the fall—just to drive through the country to see the foliage in its two most splendid stages.

"Follow the signs that say 'Bakersfield,'" the agent had advised sternly. "If it doesn't say 'Interstate 5,' don't take it. Don't be sidetracked by alternate routes or any of that stuff. You just pretend you're going all the way to Bakersfield, and you'll be all right."

After roughly twenty minutes of driving, the freeway flanked on either side with hills and homes, or flatlands and homes, or signs indicating the way to Burbank Studios or Universal City, I found myself entering a much more arid climate . . . and able to see the bank of smog I'd left behind. If there's such a thing as mountainous desert, I felt I was in the middle of it.

It was totally foreign to me to see such sharp and jagged foothills and mountains, covered with nothing but low scrub brush, and occasional scattered trees that hugged the ground as if recoiling from the heat of the sun. While it was a dry heat, my system was totally unprepared for the lack of moisture, especially in November. For miles, the stark and unyielding land, with its sharp peaks revealing shale layers ruggedly ascending at angles often steeper than forty-five degrees, held me enthralled. It took no imagination at all to realize I was definitely in earthquake country; the violent upthrust of the hills and mountains left no doubt whatsoever of how they were formed.

The four-lane freeway was reassuring to an Easterner, but the signs for the distant turnoffs could have existed only in the West: Antelope Valley Freeway, Hungry Valley Road—all that was missing was "Dead Man's Gulch." I couldn't help wondering if I should have brought a water canteen and a Winchester, but approximately every twenty-five or thirty miles, there would be a modern gas station just off the freeway at some descriptive exit. The highway was so well marked that I'd swiftly lost all concern about getting lost.

The stark terrain continued to captivate me and I wondered who in the world would live under these conditions—obviously, someone must or why would they have built such a broad freeway? The short trees and scrub seemed unending, looking very much like the whiskers on a teen-ager against the barren soil. After what seemed like endless miles of uncompromising, harsh environs, I was amused to note a sign that announced, "You Are Now Leaving the Angeles National Forest." Forest? Where? Surely even in the West they wouldn't designate such stumpiness as a forest; unless, of course, this area was but the perimeter and the trees existed elsewhere . . . ?

Ultimately, a turnoff sign called "Quail Lake Road"—though no lake was in sight—brought about a shift in the terrain. Still dry, the elevation increased considerably and the volcanic hills became more rounded, closer to our New England hills except devoid of trees or true greenery. While it was now acceptably cool, the lack of moisture in the air still pierced my lungs strangely. There was a majestic beauty of sorts to this new territory—probably its vastness more than any actual aesthetic value. Ravines and gullies made peach pits of the land, yet I felt that I could almost reach out and touch the rolling hills, sensing that they would be as soft as a horse's nose . . . yet knowing such fantasies were preposterous. After a while, following a gruelingly long and steep incline, the freeway passed a cluster of gas stations with an off-ramp sign naming the area Gorman.

Then at last, the now-familiar green of the freeway signs loomed with Frazier Park and I turned off and headed for what seemed like "town": two gas stations, an ugly squat edifice that boasted Basque food and cocktails, and a raw cement brick structure that called itself a deli. It had to be the correct direction; there seemed to be nothing on the other side of the freeway except jagged hills and sand. I pulled into the closest station and filled up—more as a precaution since it had taken very little gas to get there.

"Is this Frazier Park?" I asked the full-jowled attendant as he washed my windshield.

"Yup."

Shades of my New England upbringing! "Yes, but is this *it*? All of it?"

"No, ma'am."

I stared at the back of the man's neck, fascinated by the way the wrinkles on the back of his neck writhed with his exertion, like a snake's scales as it bellies along the sand. "Well, how do I find the rest of it?"

He nodded in the direction of the road. "Up there. 'Bout two miles. That's Frazier proper." He stopped washing the windshield and crossed over to the pump, urging a few more drops of gasoline into the tank. "Lookin' for someone special?"

For no reason I could have articulated, the man's question and tone of voice irritated me; he seemed less interested in being of help than in learning the reason for my presence, and I heard myself, with equal terseness, replying, "No, just touring." I began to feel the cold, however, and put on a sweater.

He nodded as I handed him the money for the gasoline. "Try in town. Somebody up there might help you."

The short uphill drive revealed a road sign proclaiming that this was, indeed, Frazier Park and that the population was 1,167 and the altitude was 4,610 feet. It was much closer in appearance to the land just before Quail Lake: hostile, unrelenting, and covered with scrubby bushes and trees. The soil was grayish and looked like fossilized sand; it seemed inconceivable that anything at all could grow in it. On either side of the road, a few tattered signs with faded paint invited one to stop in to visit a few realtors for tourist information, and one offered land for sale for the astounding sum of $280 per acre. I could well believe the land was going so cheaply; who'd want to buy it? And unless this area got some snow, where on earth would they get any water? Judging from the abrupt change in temperature, though, and the elevation, I rather imagined that it would snow during winters; but there was no evidence of it right then.

Finally, a sign indicated the Frazier Business District with an arrow pointing to my right. All I could see at that moment were a few old trailers, some hastily put together small houses, and a few dirt roads leading off the paved section. This gave way to a log-cabin restaurant, quite a few mechanics' garages and spare-parts businesses, a low building called the Assembly of God, a rundown place that called itself a beauty parlor, and a realtor's office. I hadn't seen any people as yet, so I decided to take advantage of the possibly outdated offer to stop in for tourist information.

Spotting a lone car parked in the rutted dirt area next to the office, I pulled in and hoped for the best. A tall, thin man was stretched out on an old naugahyde couch, reading something called *The Mountain Enterprise*, which I assumed to be their local newspaper. Hearing my footstep at the screen door, he swiftly raised himself and met me at the door. "Hi, ma'am. Welcome to Frazier."

The room was uncomfortably warm and cigar smoke hung in the air. "Thank you," I managed to say and then produced the slip of paper with Mansfield Watersdown's name and address. "I'm trying to find this gentleman," I began. "He's a retired lawyer and . . ."

"Ol' Manny? Sure I know him. Lives just up the road a bit. Known Manny long, have you?"

His smile was unctuous and I had the distinct impression that the realtor hated Mansfield Watersdown with the fierceness of the Hatfields and the McCoys. However, I was so relieved to have run down my man that I didn't permit myself the luxury of dwelling on the realtor's attitude. "No, we've never met. I have to find him for some legal advice," I offered.

The man snickered and scratched his left shoulder slowly. "Well, ol' Manny ain't practiced law in a mighty long time. You might do better to hie up to Bakersfield and find yourself a younger lawyer."

"Perhaps," I hedged, growing a bit resentful at the attitude of the only two residents I'd encountered thus far. "However, I want to talk to Mr. Watersdown for a specific reason. Can you tell me where this address is?"

"You ain't from Los Angeles, are you? You don't talk like an Angeleno . . . for that matter, not even like the folks up in Frisco."

I sighed; somewhat impatiently, I feared. "I'm from Boston."

"Well, do tell! Sure. Now I can pick it out! Boston! You're a mighty far piece from home, ain't you?" He was still scraping slowly at his shoulder and it was making me rather uncomfortable. "Anyways, I reckon you ain't come all this way to tell me 'bout your travels, right?"

"Well, I *am* rather anxious to find Mr. Watersdown," I hinted.

The thin man nodded sympathetically and brought his bony hand away from his shoulder. "C'mon outside and I'll point you in the right way." He opened the door for me, and the blast of chill air was refreshingly welcome. "Now this here's Mount Pinos Way. Now see that upholstery shop up there a piece? The place called Fred's Upholstery?"

I nodded, wrapping my arms about myself as the chill seeped through the heavy knit of my sweater. A wind had come up; not enough to do any howling, but sufficient to make it quite a bit colder.

"Well, that there's Santa Cruz Street. You turn right there, and keep followin' your nose 'til you get to the top. It's got a dirt road leadin' off to the left, but since it ain't snowed yet this year, it ain't too bad. Darnedest thing about the snows this year. Usually got it right up to your ar—, er, I mean waist-high by now. Mighty strange we ain't had none yet."

"The dirt road goes off to the left," I prodded with a smile.

"Oh yeah. You can't miss it. It'll wind up the hill a piece, an' then you'll see a small log cabin with a stone chimney.

That's ol' Manny's place. He's got a Toyota four-wheel drive up there, white and blue. Can't miss it."

"What about a telephone?" I asked, shivering uncontrollably by then. "Shouldn't I phone him first?"

"Nah. Why waste the time. 'Sides, phones don't work none too well around here anyways. You just go on up and tell Manny I said so. Hank's my name. He'll know."

I thanked Hank and got back into my rented car, hoping fervently that someone had put some antifreeze in the radiator. What a strange place California was! Sixty-six miles to the south was a sunny, balmy Los Angeles, where even a sweater wasn't necessary in mid-November. But up in Frazier, a scant hour and a half drive away, it was almost as cold as Boston.

The engine turned over right away and I got back onto the main road in Frazier, Mount Pinos Way. I passed a small structure that hailed itself as "SEARS—A complete DEPART-MENT STORE at your fingertips! Barbara Wilks, Authorized Catalog Merchant." A decent-sized market was on my left, and finally I came to the upholstery shop and turned right. True to his word, the end of Santa Cruz Street did have a dirt road on the left, and I hoped the shock absorbers of the rented car would survive as the car lurched and bounced along at less than five miles per hour. I stopped in a cloud of gritty sand and honked lightly before switching off the ignition, then got out of the car and hoped Mr. Watersdown was at home. On the other hand, I reminded myself, where else could he go in this God-forsaken place?

I waited a few moments, then saw someone appear at the front door. I couldn't really make out what the person looked like through the glass portal of the door, but I tried to smile reassuringly.

"What do you want?" a man's voice barked.

"Mr. Watersdown?"

"That's right."

"May I speak to you for a few moments? I've come all the way from Boston to find you. . . ."

There was a moment's silence and I rather guessed he was assessing me. "Who are you? What do you want?"

Clearing my throat nervously, I shouted back, "I'm Alyce

Laird, Mr. Watersdown. Juliana's daughter . . . Juliana Prather Laird."

"Juliana's daughter?" His voice sounded incredulous.

"Yes, sir. She told me to find you, to look you up," I called and produced my mother's letter, waving it to him as if, somehow, he could read the words at that distance. Yet the act served its purpose. Mr. Watersdown unbolted the door, and I could hear yet another latch being undone before the door finally swung open. In the doorway stood a man who must have been well over six feet in his prime, but was now stooped. His face was square-jawed and, though not tanned, it had the same kind of weathered look I'd become accustomed to from my mother, and the few people I'd seen in this vicinity. He wore a faded red-checkered flannel shirt and a pair of Levi's with a broad leather belt that sported a heavily tooled silver buckle. His feet were clad in heavy boots, the kind that lace up beyond the ankle, and his trousers were tucked inside their tops. All in all, Mr. Watersdown looked like some old prospector much more than he looked like a lawyer.

"Well, come in, girl, come in! Don't waste good heat letting the door stand open!"

I hesitated only a second, realizing suddenly that I felt terribly intimidated by the entire situation—or perhaps by the abruptness of these unfriendly mountain people—then quickly strode into the house while the old man held the door for me. No sooner had he closed it than he bolted it up again, then turned and looked at me intently.

"Yes," he said, staring openly, "yes, you're Juliana's girl. No two women in the world ever had those eyes unless they were mother and daughter. Your mother has eyes that can look right through you, read a man's mind. You're not as hard a woman as she is, though. I can see that. No, you're still afraid of life; your mother wasn't."

It seemed most inhospitable to me that I'd no sooner walked through the man's door and I was being analyzed, but I said nothing. After all, even if I'd had the nerve to speak up, what words could I have used that wouldn't have defeated my purpose in being there. I needed information, and his help; if it meant I had to stand there for an hour and a half while he compared me to my mother, I supposed I'd have to.

"Well, come in, girl, come in. Let's go into the parlor by the fire and warm up. I'm not as young as you are," he said, preceding me down a short hallway, "cold goes right through your bones when you're my age and sometimes you think you'll never live long enough to feel warm again. Age is a cruel thing, young lady, it rapes the mind and ravages the body."

We turned a corner and were in the parlor, where a good-sized fire burned inside its rock hearth. The room was crudely finished, as one would expect of a mountain cabin, with exposed log beams and rough mortar in hardened ooze between them. The floor was covered with scattered Indian rugs, quite old and frayed, yet keeping the chill from beneath the house at a respectable distance. A lopsided long table ran against one wall, and on top of it were numerous books and magazines, catalogues and mail—some of which looked unopened—and at least four ashtrays heaped with tobacco tampings. More Indian rugs hung from the walls at several places, to keep out the cold, I assumed, and protective storm windows were already up on the three windows overlooking the area to the north. It wasn't an especially attractive view: a lot of stumpy brush and trees, the gray sandy terrain, and a few tin rooftops.

Mr. Watersdown lowered himself into the one armchair in the room, exhaling heavily as his torso came to rest on the dull brown cushion. "If you want tea, you'll have to make it yourself," he said with a little laugh of apology. "If you want something stronger, all I've got is some cider that should be fermented enough by now."

Now that he'd convinced himself that I truly was who I claimed, his entire attitude had totally changed. He was more the cantankerous but kindly grandfather, and childhood memories of *Heidi* came to my mind. "Whatever you'd prefer, Mr. Watersdown," I said. "I'd be happy to make you some tea, if you wish. Or just tell me where you keep the cider, and I'll get it. . . ."

"Seems to me that if you're all that uncertain about your own preferences, then you don't really want anything at all. Let's talk awhile first, if you don't mind." He picked up a pipe from the sawn-off tree trunk that served as his end table and tamped fresh tobacco into it. "How's your mother?" he asked, lighting the pipe with an unsteady hand.

My face must have reflected my uncertainty about what response to give him; he was so old that I was afraid the truth might prove too great a shock.

"Well? Speak up, girl!"

"I—I'm afraid she's dead, sir," I stammered.

Mr. Watersdown closed his eyes for a moment, then nodded to himself. When he opened his eyes again, he looked at me squarely. "Tell me, Alyce," he said slowly, "from natural or unnatural causes?"

"W-what?" I truthfully didn't understand his question; it seemed so completely out of left field, I wasn't even sure I had correctly understood.

"What I'm asking you, girl, is whether or not your mother was murdered!"

"Murdered!" I echoed feebly.

"It wouldn't be the first murder in your family, young lady, and the people responsible for the last one would have a lot to gain if they could get rid of Juliana."

Realizing what he was driving at, finally, I once again took Mother's letter from my handbag and held it tentatively. "She died from a heart attack, Mr. Watersdown. I'd never known about how my father died until I was clearing away her personal effects . . . and came across this letter. It's all I know about any of it." I handed it to him.

He took it from me with his palsied hands, looking steadily into my eyes with his own clear, alert brown ones. He read through it as quickly as his trembling would permit, then folded it neatly and returned it to me. "She never was one to go rambling on," he commented, and his eyes seemed misted with some memory I could not even guess. "She sure took a lot for granted," Mr. Watersdown added after a moment, his eyes crinkling. "To send you off in search of me was the apex of optimism . . . if I had any sense at all, I'd have died years ago!"

I couldn't resist smiling. "I'm certainly glad you didn't!"

The old man puffed significantly on his pipe, eying me speculatively. "Don't be so sure, Alyce. I'm too old to be of much help to you now. I can tell you about the past, as best as

I can recollect it—but it's the future that has me worried now."

"The future?"

He nodded. "There'll be some people around here who will not be very glad to know you're in this part of the country."

"Because of my share of the estate?"

"That's only a part of it, Alyce. Even your mother never knew everything that was involved. For that matter, I'm not all that sure that *I* know."

His voice sounded tired, as if my arrival had wearied him enormously. "Well," I began, "I'm not here to make any trouble. I just want to claim what is rightfully mine, and I'll be gone."

"No doubt, no doubt. But what you think is rightfully yours, and what some other folks are going to think—well, it could be two very different things."

CHAPTER FIVE

"Maybe you'd best make some tea after all," he said, and edged his way out of the chair slowly. "I'll throw another log on the fire. Unless you're in some kind of hellfire rush, it'll take me a piece to tell you the whole story—what I know of it." With the pipe jutting from his craggy face, he seemed to lean his hands on his knees as he shuffled toward the fireplace. "Damned rheumatism really gets to me 'bout this time of year," he muttered in my general direction.

I stood up, glancing about the room, unsure of where the kitchen would be. It would be rude of me to just go in idle search of someone else's house, yet I sensed that the old lawyer would be annoyed if I inquired—I was simply supposed to know, I gathered, where everything would be.

Mr. Watersdown twisted from his stooped position and just stared at me for a second, then nodded to himself in some silent conclusion. "Behind that Indian blanket over there, on the east wall . . . nothing fancy. Hot plate's good enough for my needs. Tea's in the Folger's coffee can on the right. Pot's still on the burner, in all likelihood. Probably dirty, too."

"That's all right," I said, trying to sound at ease. "I can manage."

He nodded again, and lifted a quarter-sized log with a small grunt, then hefted it into the fire. "Well?" he inquired. "Going to stand there gawking all day?"

"No, sir," I answered swiftly, and walked across the uneven wooden floor to the east wall. I pushed aside the blanket and saw there was a wooden peg to hold it in place. One couldn't properly call it a kitchen; it was an alcove. A small refrigerator was beneath the two-burner hot plate. Above them were four unpainted shelves with canned goods stacked haphazardly, and a crude cupboard of sorts was over the heavily stained sink. It was obvious that Mr. Watersdown emptied his cold tea directly into the sink without washing it afterward. It was mottled with brownish stains, and I knew I'd have to clean it before too much time went by; that is, if I got to know Mr. Watersdown as well as I hoped I would.

I put the tin kettle on to boil the water, rinsed out the chipped teapot, and marveled at how an elderly bachelor could survive on tea and canned foods.

"If you're hungry," he called while lowering himself back into his armchair, "there's some peanut butter and crackers in the cupboard over the sink. Make yourself at home, Alyce . . . I'm too old to play the gracious host."

I smiled to myself. His entire attitude was so similar to my mother's that I found myself relaxing almost at once. They could have been brother and sister, I thought, and then wondered if perhaps it wasn't a characteristic germane to the area; that, or perhaps just the similarity of their generation. If I guessed correctly, he wasn't nearly so concerned about my own hunger as he was indirectly requesting me to bring him something to eat. Mother had always had the ability to suggest something as if she were interested in your welfare, when, in reality, she was asking a favor for herself. I pulled down the half-empty jar of peanut butter, found the box of soda crackers, and placed them on a thick crockery plate. None of the plates matched; most of them seemed chipped or even cracked. If Mother could've seen the way Mr. Watersdown lived, she would have blustered in outrage.

"Now let's see," he began. "You already know your mother had a first husband, and three offspring—issue, as we call 'em in the law."

"Are they still living?" I asked, mindful that the kettle had no whistling device and I'd have to listen for it to bubble.

"Hell yes! Alive, feisty, and somewhat tainted."

"Tainted?"

He grinned impishly, tapping the stem of his pipe against his temple. "Well, I don't mean they're crazy or anything like that," he said. "But they are rather strange, if you know what I mean."

I shook my head in bewilderment. I had no idea of what he meant, and the old devil knew it. He had to have his fun, take his time with his yarn. It occurred to me that Mr. Watersdown probably had very few visitors, if any, and he was going to enjoy this occasion to the hilt. The water was boiling and I poured it into the pot, covering it carefully so it could steep, then brought everything into the living room and placed it on the magazine-littered table between us.

"I reckon every family's got its feuds and disagreements," he continued. "Just seems that the Mussers have got more than their fair share. Melanie's about fifty-six by now, I guess. Yes, must be about that. Lives in a world of her own. Taciturn woman, a little like your mother—but without the strength of character, the will power your ma had. Doesn't matter what it is, just about everything seems to go right beyond her."

"Did you know Mother's first husband?"

"Samuel? Yes, I knew him. Staid fellow. Upright. Not very interesting. Just a hard worker. He thought the world of Juliana, though, and was good with the children. Always hoped he'd find the Lost Mine of the Padres. Never did, of course."

"Lost mine?" I asked, feeling that the narrative was getting somewhat complicated.

"Oh, just an old legend in these parts. Sam believed it. So did Melanie's beau. Strange, but both Sam and her beau died searching for that mine." Mansfield Watersdown leaned forward with obvious effort and poured each of them a cup of the steaming brew. "If you want milk with this, you're out of luck," he said good-naturedly.

"No thanks. I take it black."

"So'd Juliana. If I'd have had the sense God gave a billy goat, I'd have married her myself after Sam died." His voice trailed off. "But let's not digress. Juliana was about forty-one when Sam died. A proud woman. Stood straight and tall as a redwood. But she knew how to laugh," he added, his eyes clouding wistfully. "My yes, your mother could find the humor in just about anything. Seems to me you didn't inherit that from her," he added, his quivering hand trying to raise the cup to his lips.

"Perhaps," I replied softly, trying very hard not to sound disrespectful, "it's because I never saw that side of her. There was not much to laugh about while I was growing up."

He cocked his head to one side in a gesture that said "be that as it may," and said, "The boys sent her as much money as they could, while they still had some left to spare. Things have been pretty tight these past few years."

"Alexander and William?"

"The same. Though they're not boys anymore, of course. They live off the land. Make enough to sustain the old house and have a few amenities. But it's not the way it used to be. Alex still runs the place, just as he always has. Melanie keeps house for them both, the boys, that is."

"Didn't any of them ever marry?" I asked, sipping the strong tea. It felt warm and reassuring as it went down.

"Alex did. Other two didn't. Melanie stopped seeing other men when her intended died; daresay she's still grieving him. William, on the other hand, was always a confirmed bachelor. Must've been hard on all three of them when your mother left 'em. William was only about seventeen then. Too old to be considered a child, true; but not yet a man."

I tried to envision my mother's departure more than thirty years before. Was there a tearful farewell? Silent embracing? How does a mother leave her first three children and go off to a totally new life with the child of another marriage? What agonies had it caused all of them? I wondered if they wouldn't resent meeting me now; it would certainly be an understandable reaction.

"Now, don't go blaming yourself, young lady!"

I couldn't help a somewhat sheepish smile. "I wasn't, not really."

"So say you," he muttered. "Anyway, William keeps his father's mine working still. Still some borax in there, not an awful lot though."

"Borax!" I exclaimed. "I don't know why . . . silly, I guess, but whenever I hear the word *mine*, I always think of gold."

The old man raised his eyes heavenward. "Spare me these Easterners," he said lightly. "Child, if Sam had a gold mine, none of what came to pass would have been necessary. Sure, there's gold in these mountains. That's what ruined your mother's life, though. The shifty deal your father got involved in. Cost him his life." He paused to relight his pipe, glancing out the window as he did so. "Night's comin'. Light snowfall, too. You planning on staying over?"

I turned toward the window and saw the lazy white confetti drifting downward against the darkening sky. It seemed surreal to me. I felt as if I had been catapulted into a cocoon in time. Perhaps everything was happening too swiftly. Snowy, slushy Boston last night; balmy, sunny, palm-tree-lined Los Angeles this morning—and now, a rough log cabin in some barren mountain outpost; an old man I'd never met who knew my entire family when I didn't. In Boston, a similarly disinterested snowfall would have melted before it hit the pavement. Here, in Frazier, who knew what it portended—certainly not I. Mansfield Watersdown seemed to read my mind—again.

"Roads won't be very safe tonight, Alyce. At this altitude, surrounded by the forests, even the lightest snowfall blankets the roads in solid ice pretty fast. You'd best stay over."

"Is there a motel nearby?" I asked. For some reason, I knew I had no desire to stay in a motel; it was merely a polite question. Here I was, snugly warm with a crackling, spitting fire before me, learning things about my heritage, my history, I'd never had a chance to learn before. I'd have to be crazy to willingly leave the security of Mr. Watersdown's rough-hewn cabin.

"There is, but not much of one," he answered, bringing my attention back to the moment. "Besides, don't see any logic in you having to go to a restaurant when I've not had anybody make me a good supper in quite a spell. I'll give you bed and board, girl, in exchange for a nice, warm supper. Is that fair?"

I had to smile at his obvious strategy. "Is there anything here to cook?" I asked with a mildly teasing tone.

Mr. Watersdown snorted. "'Course there is! You don't think I live on peanut butter and crackers, do you?"

"The thought had crossed my mind," I said.

He shook his head at me in mock sternness. "Damned foolishness! I've got a fine smoke shed back of the cabin. Got rab-

bit and venison back there." His voice was grumpy, but his
dark brown eyes twinkled. "Besides," he added grudgingly,
"Mrs. Cayard brought me a fine cooked ham this morning.
That woman's got a face that would stop a rattler, but she's a
damned fine cook!"

✳❖✳

I'd finished washing up the supper dishes and pots in the
cramped kitchen, and had just taken the Ajax to the tea-
stained sink. I had decided to trek out to the shed and get a
rabbit, thinking that at least that way, Manny—we'd come to
first names during dinner—would at least have a choice of
what to eat when he had to fix his own meal the next day. I'd
never cooked a rabbit before, but I found some slightly wilted
carrots in the small refrigerator, half an onion, a jar of olives,
and a sack of sprouting potatoes in a cupboard beneath the
sink. I decided it couldn't be too hard to make a rabbit stew,
—how different could it be from beef or chicken?—and I
amazed myself with how well it turned out. Though I have always cooked my own meals, I'm not exactly a world-
renowned chef. I approach the preparation of food as if it
were a geometrical problem that has to be solved—if potatoes
taste good, and rabbit tastes good, then it follows that the
combination would be good. To that degree, I can claim some
measure of inventiveness; but I am not what could be termed
a creative person in the kitchen.

Dinner had been convivial and comfortable. I learned that
Manny had grown up in Texas, gone to law school in Hous-
ton, and had come to California as a young man. He'd passed
the California Bar and set up a practice in what was then the
Pueblo of Los Angeles in 1910. To my amazement, I learned
that Mansfield Watersdown had been the consulting attorney
for some very famous silent movie stars, and a few fly-by-
night movie studios such as Metro-Goldwyn-Mayer and Mack
Sennett. Somehow, having met this recluse in the twilight of
his life, I had a difficult time imagining him as a *bon vivant*
and highly successful lawyer in such a glamorous world.

But Manny explained that his Texas upbringing never left
him, that he had to get away to reality whenever possible, so
he built a small cabin between Frazier and Gorman for week-

end retreat. It was during that period that he'd met my mother and Samuel Musser. "Town of Gorman wasn't much more than three sticks in the wind back then," Manny had said. "Damned near had to take a mule just to get to it."

About twenty families lived within a ten-mile radius of Frazier and Gorman. From what Manny had said, the area seemed to be comprised of a hay and feed store, a saloon, a general provisions store, and a livery. "Folks kept talking about building a church someday," Manny had said, "but in those days, a man's church was in his heart—especially here in the West." However, the people did come to realize that their children were going to need an education of some kind, and they decided to convert the saloon into a schoolroom in the mornings. Those parents who knew how to read and write took turns giving the children their lessons, unless it was time to harvest the crops. Harvest time was the only vacation the children knew, but even at that, if they were old enough, they helped their parents with the chores. My own family, it appeared, grew only enough for their own use. Samuel Musser was not very interested in farming, and left those responsibilities mostly to my mother and her two sons. He, instead, preferred to work the borax mine, delivering the borax to Bakersfield four times a year.

It sounded like a terribly harsh life to me, but Manny insisted that my mother didn't mind. That she took enormous pride in growing her vegetables in a land that resisted cultivation; and that her joy was a very small rose garden in front of the porch. She was the only one who'd ever had any success with a garden in that sandy, dry soil, and she was the envy of everyone. "She could make a flower grow out of a rock!" Manny had said, smiling contentedly as he sopped up the last of his stew with a crust of bread.

It had been, for me, a charming evening. I began to see my mother in an entirely different light—to see her as a rounded human being, a woman who was close to the earth, fiercely proud and devoted to her family. I was seeing her now as Manny had seen her. And my resentment toward her harsh fate was renewed. Moreover, I felt a keen compassion for her three children.

I put away the cleanser and rinsed out the sink, my mind

churning with images of the past, marveling at how my mother had endured grimy Boston—without her rose garden. Wiping my hands on the sackcloth towel that hung from a nail, I turned to the living area. "Manny, would you introduce me to my half brothers and sister tomor . . . ?" I stopped mid-sentence as my eyes perceived Manny's slumped form in the armchair. His mouth was agape, his face highlighted by the dwindling fire in the hearth. Mansfield Watersdown was sound asleep, snoring softly.

CHAPTER SIX

I was awakened in the morning by the sound of rattling utensils and the strong aroma of coffee brewing while the re-assuring odor of bacon permeated the cabin, the rasher spitting in its pan and Mansfield Watersdown cursing back at it. I'd found a warm quilt in his bedroom, the night before, and had slept in my clothes on his couch. Although I had removed my shoes, I'd wrapped myself cocoon-like in the old blanket and had slept dreamlessly.

"You'd best wake up, Alyce," Manny called in his deep, gruff voice.

"I am," I answered, snugly warm and not anxious to leap from my repose.

"Whyn't you use my bed last night?" he questioned.

"I was pretty sure you'd wake up in the night and want to use it yourself. Mother used to doze off like that, too—usually with the TV on. She'd wake up when the hissing and crackling of nonbroadcast came on, then go to bed and go right back to sleep." The smell of his breakfast preparations was taking me back to childhood: the luxury of lying in bed and knowing that someone else had everything ready. There was a great sense of security to it, and I couldn't resist reveling in it for yet a little longer.

"Old age, I guess," he commented. "That's just what I did. Go to bed. 'Bout two or three in the morning, I guess. Didn't look. Don't have much use for clocks at my age."

I heard a fork scraping to turn the bacon over and Manny's

curse as it spluttered. "If you turn the flame down, it won't spatter so much," I suggested.

"And if you're so damned smart, you can come over here and do it!" he hurled back, but I heard the hot-plate knob being moved to a lower heat. "Bathroom's off the bedroom," he added.

I smiled. "I found it last night, thanks."

"Well, hurry up, girl. It's damned near six o'clock! I haven't got all day to fix you breakfast."

"You, sir," I replied while unwrapping myself from the quilt, "are a grouch."

He walked toward me, holding the skillet in his unsteady hand. "I'll have a bit more respect, Alyce Prather Laird! Now get in there, and be quick about it. Eggs'll be ready in just a moment."

I hastened out of the way of the precariously held skillet and impetuously gave him a morning kiss on his cheek. I don't know why, especially, maybe because I felt considerably less than my arid thirty years. I felt girlish, and warm, and, most importantly, welcome. I think Manny was shocked at my action; but he also seemed rather pleased. Scurrying to the cramped bathroom, I found that he'd laid out two clean towels for me, and a toothbrush still new in its cellophane wrapper. The old bear was, indeed, a cantankerous fraud.

Returning to the eating area, Manny was just breaking two eggs into the greased skillet. I walked to the window and gasped at what I saw. The sun was now well over the horizon, a burnished gold filtering over a world that had turned to marshmallow in the night. No longer was the vista one of a tawdry, merciless country; now it was gracefully downy, enshrouded in the softness of a heavy snowfall. The ugly cabins I'd noticed yesterday now seemed Tyrolean, almost like a crèche in the wilderness.

"Takes your breath away, doesn't it?" Manny said softly.

I could do no more than nod to his question.

"It's what keeps me here and not in Palm Springs. I live for each winter," he added. "When you get to my age, know the end can come any day, you get to feeling that you've got to fill your eyes with the majesty of nature—as if, perhaps, the memory of it all will comfort you in the grave. There's a need, when you're old, to sort of store up everything you can. Maybe that's why," Manny chortled, "we don't like to go to bed—you never can be sure you'll wake up again."

"Oh, Manny, how can you say that! You're in excellent health," I began, turning to face him.

His shaking hands poured out the coffee into two brown mugs. "I'm eighty-nine, girl. As a friend of mine once said, 'I've reached my quota.' C'mon," he interrupted himself, "let's have breakfast and then I'll see if that damned telephone works."

"Telephone?"

"Well, are you spending your holidays with me, or did you not come here to meet your kin!" He sat down, looking at me as if I'd gone absolutely mad, then reached for a piece of bread and plunged it into his egg yolk.

✳❖✳

Fortunately, the road crews had been out early and Manny's four-wheeler gripped the tarmac efficiently. Despite his age and the ice patches, Manny drove the vehicle with a strong hand. He'd been doing a great deal of prattling since we'd started off, but I sensed it was to prevent me from becoming nervous about meeting my relatives after all those years.

"They're not a bad lot," he offered after a rundown on each's respective faults.

I had to laugh. "Are you quite sure?"

He reached over and patted my arm. "Well, you wouldn't catch me living with them, but that doesn't mean very much. I wouldn't live with *any*one!"

We'd left the small community area by then, the little shops huddled together, and had been on the highway going straight into Los Padres National Forest. Now it truly was a forest with pines outstretched toward the morning sun, capped like sundaes with the freshly fallen snow. It didn't seem as if we'd driven even three miles from Manny's cabin, and yet we were locked in a winter wilderness that defied my Easterner's credulity. Though I'd never been to the Black Forest, I imagined it must be very nearly the same. From time to time, small animals seemed to scurry across the snow but they were too far from us for me to discern if they were jack rabbits or squirrels. The entire terrain glistened as if it had been sprinkled with sequins, and the air was sharp and chilling to the lungs.

My thoughts wandered to the imminent meeting with the Mussers. From what Manny had told me, only Alexander's son, Benjamin, would be about my own age; Manny had guessed him around thirty-three years old. "Don't know very much about Ben," he'd said. "He's not openly rude, but seems to have his mind elsewhere whenever you talk to him. Maybe that's 'cause he's tired of listening to his father telling him what to do all the time."

"Does he have a profession?" I had asked.

"You mean work?" His laughter at my question was basically answer enough. "You might say that. He's a professional son. Whatever Alexander tells him to do, he does."

"In other words," I had chided, "you think he's spineless."

"As a jellyfish!"

Manny turned off the main road, interrupting my thoughts, and we were suddenly bouncing along an uneven ribbon in the terrain. I didn't know if it was a dirt road beneath the snow, or merely one in serious disrepair, but whatever the advantages of the four-wheeler, it was obviously not designed for a smooth ride regardless of surface. I clung to the dash for support as Manny pushed the vehicle at a smart thirty mph along the rutted pathway, mindless to the fact that at no time were all four wheels on the ground simultaneously. I was being jostled so badly I feared for the endurance of my bra straps. "Manny," I said after a few moments of pounding, "wouldn't it be better if we slowed down a little?"

"Be there in a minute, just hang on."

True to his word, we soon swung around a curve marked by a stone pillar, made from innumerable rocks and held together with mortar, and bounced along beyond a stand of trees. Manny turned his weathered face toward me and grinned sardonically. "There it is, right up ahead. The Musser spread."

I turned my face from him to peer through the windshield. Directly ahead, perhaps another fifty yards, was a sprawling hacienda—or, at least, what I assumed was one. It appeared to be built of stucco, with a veranda stretching across the entire frontage. I couldn't tell whether it had a tile roof or not since it was covered by snow. A huge oak door dominated the façade, and arched windows dotted the structure on either side. It appeared to be a single story in front, with a second story beginning well back from it. I couldn't tell whether this was due to the mountainous terrain, or if there was a first floor beneath it. Obviously, the house must have been quite magnificent in its day, but it showed its age now and was badly in need of some repairs and a coat of paint.

"Belonged to a Spanish don before California was admitted to the Union," Manny informed me. "Alexander's into all sorts of litigation over the place," he added, his tone betraying a certain glee over the matter.

"Why?"

A sly grin spread across his face. "Alex says he bought it, has a deed, and that it's his. Government's got another idea. Claim it belongs to the state and that the sale was invalid."

"You mean that after paying for the place, my brother could be thrown out?" I was appalled at the possibility.

Manny shrugged. "Things aren't as clear cut and simple out here as they are in the East. The history of California is pretty checkered. Owned by the Spanish, then the Mexicans, and for a while, Russia owned a lot of California."

"Russia!" I blustered.

"Fur trapping was big business in the old days. No, you can't judge California by eastern standards, Alyce. The territory's changed hands too many times. Land grants and deeds keep a lot of lawyers busy . . . even to this day."

"Are you handling his case?" I asked.

Manny glanced at me briefly. "Hell no! Let the old buzzard fight his own battles! Well, here we are," he said as he skidded to a stop in front of the house.

Even as he pulled the brake, the front door opened and a woman was coming out to greet us. She could only be Melanie, I knew, yet she was not at all what I had expected. A smile of welcome was on her face, and there was an air of expectant bustling about her. She came down the lopsided stairs at a brisk pace, holding her long woolen skirt just to her ankles to avoid tripping. Even as I opened the door of the car, I could hear her calling, "Alyce! Alyce!"

I climbed down, and found myself engulfed in Melanie's embrace, could feel her tears wet against my cheek. "Land sakes alive, Alyce!" she exclaimed after a moment. "Let's just have a look at you now." She stepped back to arm's length, still resting her hands on my shoulders. Melanie was on the plump side, but it was easy to see she must have been quite a beauty in her day. Cherub-like face, cheeks as rosy as a girl's, framed by closely cropped, gray curly hair. Her eyes were a very pale blue, and almost perfectly round, like a doll's. The face was finely wrinkled, but she had the Prather eyebrows—straight across. She looked like the wife of an Irish innkeeper, or a figure out of one of Brueghel's paintings. Somehow, perhaps influenced by Manny, I had rather expected a sinister woman: a stern brunette dressed in black. Melanie looked as if she'd be much more at ease baking bread than haunting the hallways with hands twisting upon each other in eternal anguish.

Her eyes began to tear again as she gazed at me intently. "Oh, Manny, do you see her?" she asked, her gaze never leaving my face. "It's Mamma. You are Mamma all over again!"

"Yes, Melanie, I saw it right away. But she's not Juliana, she's Alyce. And we're both about to freeze right to this spot if you don't let us go inside."

I was surprised at his tone with her; he spoke as if she were a little girl who wasn't too terribly bright. He was gentle, but there was an edge of impatience in his voice. Not the gruff manner he took with me—which I'd come to expect and understand—but as if Melanie were irresponsible and it irritated him.

"Oh, yes, I'm so sorry, my dear. Manny, you're so right, as always," she sighed good-naturedly. "Come in, child, come in. We're all just dyin' to get to know you, to have news of Mamma. It's been so long! Almost thirty years!"

Melanie placed a rounded arm about my waist and drew me up the stairs and into the house itself, with Manny trailing behind mumbling to himself. There was no actual foyer, which surprised me a little; one simply entered the living room. As we crossed the threshold, a tall well-built man strode toward us. His hair was graying at the temples, but otherwise was so dark a brown as to appear black. His poise and stance was that of a land baron, and when he reached us, he looked down at me and stared openly. "When Manny telephoned this morning, I thought you might be an imposter . . . but your resemblance to Mother is amazing."

Manny was stomping his boots free of snow just inside the doorway. "Why should she be an imposter, Alex? Got more money than you're admitting?" He almost snorted with his jibe.

"Trouble with you," Alex said severely, but not in anger, "is that you're a lawyer who doesn't practice law! There is, after all, the matter of our family legacy!" He turned toward me, brushing Melanie aside brusquely, and escorted me to the faded chintz couch. "Forgive me, Alyce, but I'm sure you understand why I'd be concerned over such a thing. Mother must have told you about how your father was swindled."

"Now, Alexander, do we have to bore the girl with all that right now? Can't we at least get to know each other a little better first?" Melanie complained, primly lowering herself into an overstuffed chair with a throw cover on it.

Manny had managed to place himself directly in front of the walk-in fireplace, letting his hands rest against the rock surface below the timber mantel. "Seems to me, as a nonpracticing lawyer that is, that the legacy's Alyce's—not yours."

It was such a harsh, unexpected comment that I felt the blood rushing to my face with embarrassment. "Manny! That's a terrible thing to say!" I glanced from Melanie's perplexed face to Alexander's scowl. "Naturally anything that belonged to Mother belongs to all of us. I've never entertained any other thought!"

"Of course not, my dear. It's just Manny's, uh, shall we say, sense of humor?" He took a high-backed chair opposite me and looked for all the world like a man who should be wearing English hunting boots. A full-chested man, he had something of a military bearing about him; yet there was an aura of self-effacing hardship, a depth to his eyes that belied his outer appearance. A kind of martyrdom seemed to lurk in the shadows of his pupils.

"But perhaps Melanie is right," Alexander went on, "let's do get to know each other before all the unpleasantness has to be discussed."

Manny turned from the fireplace and rubbed the small of his back contentedly. "She doesn't have much information about it anyhow," he said, "which is why I've brought her here. Alyce could've found her way by herself, I'm sure, if it were just a social call."

Alexander's eyebrows knitted with annoyance. "The directions to this house do not change with the purpose of the visit, Manny."

"You don't say," Manny retorted, obviously having a marvelous time baiting Alexander. "Don't you have anything to drink around here?" he asked abruptly.

"Why Mansfield Watersdown," Melanie chirped with feigned shock. "It's *only* eleven in the morning!"

Manny pursed his lips, sending a wink in my direction. "Well, now, seems to me a little touch of sherry never hurt anyone—and this is a reunion, after all. Calls for a celebration. Just to break the ice, so to speak."

Fond as I had come to be of Manny, I really felt that his levity was out of place at this moment in time. Yet, he was so obviously having a splendid time at Alexander's cost, I couldn't bring myself to be truly upset. However, the thought of a bracing sherry did appeal to me. It was a terribly uncomfortable situation to meet one's siblings after so long a time, especially since they apparently questioned how I felt about Mother's share of my father's moneys.

"Alexander, dear . . ." Melanie faltered.

"Come on, Alex, don't be so damned stingy! Break out the bottle," Manny coaxed. "Probably turned to vinegar by now anyway!" He glanced at me and smiled innocently.

Alexander Musser glared sternly at Manny, then turned a softer expression toward me. "You'll have to forgive Manny's abominable manners," he said quietly. "Senility, you know."

I saw Manny's body draw itself up to full height in silent outrage, and scored one for Alex. But I decided to keep my opinions to myself; their quarrelsomeness was obviously of long standing, and probably quite harmless. Manny was being outrageous, and the old rake knew it.

Alexander nodded to Melanie to fetch the sherry, and then turned back to me. "And Mother? Manny said she'd passed on only recently. . . . Painlessly?"

"Considering," I replied. "She suffered a heart attack, but lingered only for three days. I think she was ready to die."

"Did she speak of us often?" Alexander prodded, his amber-colored eyes searching out mine.

"Hell! Alyce didn't even know you existed until after Juliana died!"

"Manny!" I admonished. "That was not only cruel, but not really true!"

Fortunately, Melanie returned to the living room at that moment, bearing a badly chipped silverplate tray with a sherry decanter and four glasses. "Land sakes, but I had to wash the glasses before we could use them," she interrupted merrily. "Must be at least since last Christmas that we've had any sherry!" She set the tray down with an air of accomplishment.

"What *is* the truth, Alyce?" Alexander asked, leaning forward in his chair. "Did you or didn't you know of our existence?"

I tried as hard as I could to let my eyes cushion the information; it couldn't have been pleasant to learn that his own mother had rarely spoken of her first family. "Try to understand, Alex," I began falteringly. "Your mother and my mother occupied the same body, but the similarity ended there. She'd become taciturn and . . . well, and rather secretive. Now that I have found out about how my father died and all the rest, I understand why." I glanced at Manny in hopes he would help me out of this awkward situation. He was obviously still smarting from my accusation; I was on my own. "I knew that you three existed, but my information ended right there. Mother would never discuss any of you in detail; never explain why she'd moved to Boston. I'd ask, of course, as any child would—but her mouth would draw into a tight line, and I knew I'd learn nothing more."

Melanie's eyes had not left my face while I fumbled for a humane explanation. "Alyce dear? You mean to say Mamma *never* talked about us? Not even me, her first daughter?"

"Pour the sherry, Melanie," Alexander said gently. "Go on, Alyce."

I shrugged. "There's not much more to tell you, really. Up until her death, and finding that letter to me, I had no idea of how my father died, or why we never heard from any of you—much less anything about any fortune we'd been swindled out of. Obviously, Mother felt it best that I know nothing of our past while I was growing up. She was very nearly a . . . a broken spirit while I was maturing—though I never thought so at the time. We spoke of nothing intimate, Alex, but obviously leaving you three behind took a terrible toll on her. . . ." What else could I say? On the defensive, and totally unprepared to cope with the turn of the conversation, I watched and waited while Alexander's big, gnarled hands loosened their grip on the arms of the chair. I wanted to say something more, anything to break the tension and the obvious hurt in Alex's eyes, but no words would come to mind.

Melanie handed me the sherry-filled glass, slowly moving her head from side to side. "But I just don't understand, Alyce. Mamma was always so full of fun, always so warm and lovin' to us. It just defies belief that she'd not ever speak of us."

"Then the reason for coming out here . . ." Alex began.

"Is to learn the truth," Manny finished for him. "Show Alex the note Juliana left for you, girl. Let him see for himself just what brought you all the way out here."

Removing the folded letter from my handbag, I handed it over to Alex. Melanie had, in the meantime, resumed her seat and was still wearing her pleasant, expectant smile. "Did Mamma still have that glorious thick hair of hers?"

I smiled at Melanie; she was indeed like a child. If something seemed unpleasant, she would change the subject to more uplifting thoughts. "Yes," I lied, "she did."

"Just like yours," she remarked, admiration glowing in her voice. "I used to brush it for her when I was little. She was so nice to me about that . . . just sit still and let me brush her hair for*ever*, it seemed."

Alex had finished Mother's brief epistle and folded it up again. "Obviously, you really don't have any background information at all."

"I'm afraid not. I was hoping the three of you would be kind enough to help me."

"William will be at the mine all day, Alex, did you forget that?"

"The kind of help Alyce requires," Alex said softly to her, "will be prolonged. William will do as he's told."

"Of course, dear," Melanie chirped. "I wasn't entirely too sure just what kind of help it was."

"That's all right, Melanie, just let us take care of it," he explained. "Well, Alyce, I think the most logical step is for you to stay here with us for a while. We've plenty of room, and while I can tell you what happened in a relatively brief period, if you plan to try to regain your father's share of that mine, you'd best do it right here. Don't you agree, Manny?"

"I was counting on you to suggest it, Alex. There's not a thing anyone can do legally, as you know. So if the culprits are to be tripped up, confounded into a confession or whatever, they're all right here in Frazier."

"That's very kind of you, but . . ." I began.

"No, no!" Alex said. "It's the only way. And don't forget, I'm not being entirely selfless—we've a stake in this matter as well."

"But I've checked into a hotel in Los Angeles, all my luggage, everything . . ."

He waved aside my protests. "I'll send Ben into town to check you out and bring back your things."

"Did I hear my name mentioned?"

A young man had entered the living room from behind me, and the unexpected tenor voice startled me. Turning quickly, I could see that he was nothing at all like his father. Dark complexioned, about five-foot-eleven, with a crown of curly dark brown hair, almost bony in build, young Ben looked effete and a little too serious for a man his age. He came toward me and sat down on the couch, one hand loosely closed on his lap.

"You must be Alyce," he said quietly, looking at me with intense brown eyes. "Do you like animals?"

"Yes," I replied, feeling a certain alarm growing within me.

Ben's face seemed to draw some inner charge, some kind of strange delight in my reply, which baffled me at first. Slowly, he extended his hand to just in front of me, then uncurled his fingers.

"His name's Igor."

I cringed at what I saw, inwardly wanting to scream, but

knowing in some primal precognition that to do so would be a bad mistake. Igor was a baby snake. It lay across Ben's palm, writhing, then began to encircle his fingers. I wanted desperately to run, to get away from the horrible little creature, but was rooted to the spot. When I looked from the snake to Ben's face, Ben's eyes were glinting malevolently; a perverse thrill seemed to curl his lips.

What had I let myself in for?

CHAPTER SEVEN

"How many times do I have to tell you not to bring those damned things up into the house, Ben!" Alexander's face was crimson with anger, the veins in his neck standing out like rope around a trunk.

Ben took his hand and Igor away from my face, glancing at his father with an innocent air of forgetfulness.

"Are you never going to learn?" Alex added, then looked toward me with genuine embarrassment on his dignified face. "Ben fancies himself a herpetologist."

"No I don't," Ben contradicted, smiling at me with a boyish charm. "I am simply interested in all the unusual creatures of this earth. Other people have domesticated pets . . . I have all sorts of truly interesting living things. Butch, my king snake, is nearly two feet long . . . he's a beauty! Would you like to see him? I'll feed him a mouse, if you like; it's fascinating to watch him corner a field mouse and eat him."

I was in immediate danger of losing my breakfast, and I was positive all the blood in my face must have dropped to my ankles. I was searching for some sort of diplomatic way to decline when Melanie interjected and saved my verbal neck.

"Well, I just think all those, those *things*, are disgusting and I'll never know why you just sit around playing with them! A grown man, Ben, just doesn't do that!" She took a sip of her sherry as if to seal her thought.

"Nothing about life is disgusting," Ben countered, "unless it's small minds."

Manny had wisely not entered into the discussion, but instead seemed to be intently studying the ceiling as if uncertain that the exposed redwood beams would hold for yet another fifteen minutes. Melanie's lips had compressed into a rigid scar, and Alex was rubbing his eyes in an obvious attempt to regain control over the situation and himself. I had decided to try to remain on the outside of this family matter—if I possibly could.

"Ben," Alex began after a moment, "if Alyce wants to see your collection in the cellar, I'm sure she'll let you know. In the meantime, I've invited her to stay with us for a while."

The young man turned to look at me, his eyes peering into mine as if to search out if I had been crazy enough to accept.

"I want you to drive into Los Angeles," Alex resumed, "and check her out of the hotel. Get her luggage, and be back here as quickly as you can."

Ben brightened. "Alone?"

His father nodded wearily, and I could begin to see why Alexander Musser had that lurking martyrdom in his eyes. With Melanie being little more than a child, and his only son an obvious misfit, it must have been quite a burden for the older man. I really felt that it would not be a terribly bright idea for me to stay with them; with grumpy, lovable Manny, perhaps—if he'd let me—but the Mussers were indeed a strange lot and I wasn't at all comfortable with the prospect of staying in their home indefinitely. "I—I have the car to worry about," I said hesitantly.

"What car?" Alex asked.

"The rented one I came here in," I replied. "It's not so long a drive that I couldn't come up here when necessary. Just stay at the hotel until I've learned enough to justify staying up here for a longer period." I knew I wasn't sounding too logical, but I simply felt terribly apprehensive about staying with the Mussers. And Ben's . . . collection.

Alex shook his head slowly. "No, that wouldn't work. Besides, it would be horrendously expensive for you. To accomplish your mission, you have to be here in Frazier. Kyle Prescott and Juan Melendez are both right here."

"They're your father's partners' sons," Manny explained to my unvoiced question.

"My that sounds complicated," Melanie said.

Manny nodded in acknowledgment, then smiled at my perplexed expression. "Your father had two partners in the mine. They're the ones who we suspect of having murdered him, and driving your mother from Frazier—not to mention keeping all the money for themselves."

"You suspect?" I asked. "Mother was much more positive than that in her letter."

"That's because Manny is a lawyer," Alex said. "No one is ever a murderer, he's an alleged murderer, or an alleged thief. The law's a cowardly vocation, Alyce. You never hear a lawyer referring to anyone as an out-and-out crook, only that someone was convicted for a crime. Always leaving themselves a way out to avoid libel. But I agree with Mother. I was old enough at the time to have a very good grasp of the situation. There's no 'suspicion' involved in this matter! I know perfectly well Melendez and Prescott murdered your father in cold blood, and threatened our mother sufficiently for her to flee, to abandon her home, her oldest children, and run for her life."

"But you can't prove it, Dad. Right?"

"Not only can't he prove it," Manny threw in, "but the statute of limitations passed ages ago. Without an absolute confession, written or witnessed, you've nothing to go on but suspicion." Manny rolled back on his heels, his dark eyes glinting with the satisfaction of driving home his point.

"Alyce is the spitting image of our mother," Melanie said to Ben.

"Be that as it may," Alex retorted to Manny's remark, "I think Alyce stands a better chance of proving the evil that was done than the rest of us."

"Why's that?" Manny asked.

"Because she's a young and lovely woman, and because Kyle and Juan are about her age—and bachelors."

My head was beginning to spin as I followed their conversation. Inwardly, I found myself somewhat amused at the whole ludicrous situation. The culprits themselves were now dead, the statute of limitations had been exceeded, but I was supposed to seduce two young men into confessing to their fathers' criminal actions. It was preposterous! Alyce Prather Laird, the virgin Mata Hari?

"Y'know," Manny said, "it might work at that. Guess I'm past the age of thinking about handsome young studs around a pretty young girl. You may have something, Alex. You just might."

"What, may I ask," I opened cautiously, still half-amused at their role-playing game, "leads either of you to think that the two sons know anything about their fathers' actions?"

"Hmm?" Alex intoned distractedly.

"I mean, murder and chicanery would hardly have been a subject at the dinner table. Perhaps neither gentleman knows anything about what transpired so long ago. If they're about my age, they wouldn't remember anyway."

Ben sniggered at his father's surprised expression, opening his hand slightly, and whispering, "That stumped him, Igor!"

"Girl's got a point, Alex," Manny said, then turned to me. "You've got a clear logical mind, young lady. I can respect that in a fellow lawyer, but you don't often find it in a young woman."

"Well, how else are we going to find out whether they know anything or not!" Alex retorted, aggravation written on his face. "That's why Alyce will be so valuable to us all. If she can obtain the confidence of either Kyle or Juan—or both of them, for that matter, play them off as rivals—then we'll know how to proceed." Alexander ended on a firm note of triumph, then moved over to the tray and poured himself some more sherry. As a second thought, he refilled my glass, then Manny's. "Want some?" he said to Ben, his voice revealing disapproval.

Ben merely shook his head, slouching down into the couch, clenching and unclenching his fist in some form of petting the baby snake it contained.

Manny drew a trembling, arthritic hand across his chin. "If they *do* know something, that could put Alyce in a dangerous position," he mused aloud, then he grinned broadly. "But if they don't, one of them'll probably propose anyhow—so it's about the same thing. She'll still have the money she was supposed to have."

"Wouldn't it be fun to have a wedding!" Melanie laughed.

No one seemed to pay any attention to her remark. Now I was supposed to get married as well? I was beginning to have grave thoughts about the wisdom of having come to California. None of that entire conversation could possibly have taken place in Boston! I had heard of regional differences, but this was becoming too illogical for acceptance. I sensed it, I knew it somewhere in the back of my head, but I found myself unable to articulate it.

I'd been in the state less than forty-eight hours, a staid and proper Bostonian, retiring and a little shy; now suddenly I was being catapulted into a manipulative role of spy, temptress, and prospective wife. Mentally, I opened my mouth to protest; but in actuality, nothing of the sort transpired. Perhaps it was the influence of the stronger personalities about me; possibly, the sheer absurdity of me in the role held a perverse fascination for me.

After all, I'd come to California to learn the truth of my past—ideally, to reclaim my rightful share of a great deal of money. I'd embarked the plane with an attitude of adventure, of avowance to emerge from my dull shell and become a new, more confident individual. I'd sworn a new tombstone for my mother, and a new life for me. What was so terrible about the plan? I asked myself. If neither of the men knew anything, nothing awful could possibly happen to me beyond a fascinating leave of absence from my job at the college. Wasn't that what I'd wanted?

And, should it develop that either man did know the truth, was perpetuating the crime by concealment of the facts and denying me my birthright—what then? Had I not been a fool by coming to California without a plan? What was I supposed to do? Walk up to a stranger in Frazier and say, "Look here, you owe me an enormous amount of money after what you did to my father and mother, so I expect you to pay up or I'll . . ." I'll what? Cry? Tell Mansfield Watersdown on you?

No. I had childishly come to Frazier with no formulated plan. I'd not written first to verify that Mr. Watersdown was still alive, or to provide me with the addresses of my siblings. I'd just boarded a plane and flown off, with nebulous romantic notions of accomplishing something positive. I had not be-

haved at all intelligently, much less maturely. What other
plan could possibly work beyond what Alex had in mind? I
turned the question over in my mind, rapidly trying to find
any holes in its fabric—and could not. Nor could I proffer a
better proposal. And simply because their fathers might have
been accomplices in murder did not mean that the men held
similarly criminal and violent tendencies. Yet . . . and yet, my
mind recoiled from the plan, from the idea of being used as a
decoy. There was something about the scheme that frightened
me, filled me with a growing apprehension.

". . . May as well, don't you think?" Alex was saying to me.

"I'm sorry," I mumbled. "I—I'm afraid my mind was wandering."

Manny clucked in irritation. "Alex and I have worked out
the logistics of this matter, Alyce. You'll drive back to Los Angeles in your rented car, and Ben will follow you in his. The
two of you can take care of the hotel, getting your luggage,
and returning the rental car. Then you'll drive back with Ben.
It's quite simple."

I felt trapped, coerced into a commitment I'd not yet totally
accepted. Especially since Manny seemed to be in such de-
tailed accord with the direction of my life. I felt as if my
thirty years of existence had just been placed in a vase, all
neatly and prettily displayed, and I was merely to serve as
decor for someone else's living arrangements. I was not to be
functional so much as a distraction, a diversionary tactic.

Somewhere in Frazier, two men were going about their
lives—possibly innocent men, possibly guilty . . . perhaps
even dangerous. I was elected to be the snare to establish the
truth. The scene in that room seemed unreal to me, even
threatening. "B-but," I blurted suddenly, "what about the
statute of limitations, the, the . . ."

Manny waved my protest aside. "You get a confession, or
even a scrap of evidence like old letters, files, anything—we'll
take care of the rest."

Ben was smiling at me, a taunt in his strange eyes.

Melanie sat pertly on her chair, her bright blue eyes following from speaker to speaker.

Alex had risen and was standing by the windows at the far

end of the room, gazing out across the snow-covered terrain. "It's past lunchtime, Melanie. Why don't you fix up something for all of us. Then Alyce and Ben can head toward town."

"A sound plan," Manny volunteered.

If I had any choices, I failed to see them.

CHAPTER EIGHT

The drive back to Los Angeles seemed endless. With Ben's car directly behind me, I would have hoped to have felt a degree of security, of companionship in the knowledge that I was not totally alone in an alien land. The snow thinned out and, in a few miles, totally disappeared. There was very little traffic at that hour, yet every time I glanced into the rear-view mirror, there was Ben's dark green sedan—doggedly behind me. I changed lanes twice just to see what would happen; Ben changed right with me. He was driving entirely too close to the rear of my car, as if he could read my inner fears and mood, in rigid determination to let nothing come between us. Indeed, I didn't have the impression that a friend was following me to Los Angeles; I felt as if I were being pursued, hunted in a concrete maze with no chance of escape.

I told myself over and over that I was being silly, that there was no reason to have this reaction. Yet I found myself having to force my hands to relax their tight grip on the steering wheel, to let my shoulders return to their normal posture. By the time we reached the area known as Saugus, my entire being was so tense that I began to worry about myself. It wasn't a heart-pounding, clammy fear; it was more akin to the bodily reaction to dampness and cold—a tensing against the elements.

Soon, the familiar palm trees began to appear off the horizon of the six-lane freeway; apartment houses became visible, schools, unlit neon signs for shopping plazas and banks—at least I was back in civilization, though the squatness of the area still amazed me. I turned on the car radio for company, hoping it would aid me to relax. Flipping the dial, I was amused at the number of country-western programs, came to a couple of jarring and blaring rock-'n'-roll stations, and finally found a classical music program.

Freeway signs abounded, as did the accompanying decisions. From the Golden State Freeway at Frazier, dozens of alternate freeways—or so it seemed—were designated at subsequent turnoffs. It was like a science-fiction story. I was a nucleus, the automobile was my protoplasmic cell; together we would forevermore course through the cement arteries of a mammoth, palpitating creature known as El Pueblo de Los Angeles. It was bizarre. I knew my imagination was getting the better of me, but when I saw the sign that said, "HOLLYWOOD: Next Seven Exits," I felt a definite sense of relief. Turning off on Highland Avenue, just past the Pilgrimage Theatre, and driving by the Hollywood Bowl, I almost felt as if this had always been my home. It was busy, there were pedestrians again—I was back in the world . . . with Ben right behind me.

Since the car rental agency was directly across the street from the Roosevelt Hotel, I decided to turn the car in first; it would be simpler than trying to find a parking place. Ben waited in his sedan, never waving or smiling—just waiting. I felt like a criminal, being tailed by the FBI. It was silly of me, and I had absolutely no reason for feeling guilty or hunted, yet I did.

Moments later, we entered the lobby and Ben stood slightly behind me as I told the desk clerk I would be checking out. I paid for the room with a traveler's check, and folded my receipt and the change inside my handbag. "I'll go up and pack, Ben," I said, turning toward him, trying to keep the tightness out of my voice. "Why don't you get a paper and wait for me here in the lobby?"

Ben grinned and shook his head. "I'll come with you."

"I'm not a little girl, Ben. I can manage quite well by myself."

Again, that stoic, cold smile and the shaking of his head. Argument, I saw, would be valueless. His attitude angered me somewhat, but I didn't know how to handle the situation. By then, I had the distinct feeling that, if he could, Ben would have placed handcuffs on me. He frightened me, but I didn't know what to do about it. Scream? He hadn't *done* anything; what would be the purpose? It was perfectly obvious that Ben had pegged me correctly: I was timid, easily cowed by a stronger personality. While I didn't like this aspect of my character, I'd led too sheltered a life to be otherwise. My psyche screamed silently; I wanted to be assertive enough, aggressive enough to command Ben to do as I'd said. But the right words simply would not come to mind, nor could I have uttered them if they had.

With indignant frustration, I turned on my heel and paced to the elevators. Ben, with his long bony hands thrust into his pockets, followed me in silence. Once inside my room, he sat mutely at the small writing desk, his large brown eyes following my every movement as I packed my suitcases. It made me so nervous that I kept dropping things, or packing too hastily for wrinkle-free clothing later. If only he would say something, anything! But he didn't. He just sat . . . and watched. Ben was like a sadistic jailer, just waiting for his prisoner to make a wrong move so he could "punish" him.

Just as I was finishing with the last suitcase, Ben reached into his pocket and pulled Igor out, placing the small snake on top of the desk.

I shuddered involuntarily. Why did Ben feel it necessary to torment me in this manner? I was certain he knew what effect the squirming thing had upon me; that and Ben's smirking silence were going to drive me berserk. I remembered reading somewhere that young rattlers are terribly dangerous, and that one should not be deceived by their size. As I recalled, even a very young rattlesnake has already attained nearly its adult degree of lethal venom. I didn't know if this would be true of Igor, still small enough to fit into a pocket—but I had no intentions of finding out.

I closed the two locks on the suitcase, and walked over to the bedside telephone, summoning the bellboy to come for my luggage. Glancing at my wristwatch, I was taken aback to see it was already past four o'clock. I returned the receiver to its cradle, and found myself drawn to watch Igor writhing across the desk. In that brief moment, I felt myself nearly mes-

merized by the creature. The unexpected ringing of the telephone jolted me rather badly, and Ben snickered as I pulled
myself together and answered it.

"Long-distance call for you, Miss Laird."

"Me?" I said inanely. But the operator didn't reply, and instead merely made the connection.

"Alyce? Is that you?"

I almost blubbered with pleasure and the relief from the
day's tension. "Tharon Ann!" I blurted.

"Well! You certainly have put me through a lot of worry!
Where have you been, Alyce?"

Her anger was not real, I knew, though I could tell from
her staccato delivery that she had been concerned. "Up in
Frazier, meeting my family."

"You've found them already? So soon?" she cried.

"Yes," I replied, glancing briefly at Ben. "In fact, my nephew
is with me now. He's driving me back to Frazier this afternoon." Ben winced at the term "nephew," but it was the
only accurate term I could come up with—even if he was a
few years older than I.

"Well, honey, what's your address up there? Honestly,
Alyce, I just don't like all of this! I think you're crazy! You
don't know these people! Maybe they're all a bunch of Charlie
Mansons or something!"

Ben's face had resumed its quiet smirk and Tharon Ann's
words went through me like an icicle. I tried not to let my
voice reveal the terror her words had just instilled. "The address? Wait a second, let me ask Ben. Ben's my nephew," I
stated slowly and distinctly. It may have seemed strange to
Ben, but I wanted Tharon Ann to remember the name;
though I wasn't totally certain of just why it was so vitally important to me. I left the mouthpiece uncovered as I asked him
how one would address a letter to me in Frazier.

He shifted lazily in his chair, a defiance in his movement
that seemed to ask, Who in the world would ever write to
you? But finally he answered. "Care of Musser, El Fin del
Camino, Frazier, California."

"That's all?" I asked. "No street address?"

"The name of the ranch is enough."

"What does it mean?"

Ben laughed lightly. "The end of the road. Appropriate, don't you think?"

I pulled my eyes from his probing gaze and repeated the address to Tharon. "Now, don't hesitate to be in touch if you need me," I said loudly to her. "And if the college needs me for anything, you be sure and tell them where to find me, Tharon."

"Honey, is everything all right? You . . . you're sounding a little strained, not yourself."

"No, no. I'm fine, Tharon. Maybe still a little tired from the flight, but I'm really fine. But if—if anything should happen, uh, you know where I am." The knot of tension began to form in the pit of my stomach again, and I was loath to let Tharon Ann off the telephone.

"Well, all right, Alyce. But you be in touch with me. If you're short on cash, reverse the charges. But I want to know where you are and that everything's okay."

"That's awfully good of you, Tharon. I really appreciate it," I said, my free hand curling and looping through the telephone cord in nervous apprehension. Ben had picked up a pen and was poking it at Igor, taunting the snake. There was a cruel gleam in his eye as he did it.

"I've gotta go now, honey. Harry'll kill me when the bill comes in. But I was getting very worried when you weren't in yesterday or last night. When I called again this morning, and you still weren't there, well, I thought one of those Hollywood suede-shoe boys had grabbed you and mugged you."

Nothing that obvious, I thought, but didn't say. I again reassured Tharon Ann that I was fine, repeated the address in Frazier, and then said good-bye. When I looked back toward Ben, Igor had curled himself around the pen and was looking very much like a medical emblem. It seemed a playful thing for the snake to have done, almost whimsical. For a second, I forgot my fear of snakes and smiled at the picture he presented. "What made you call him Igor?" I asked Ben.

He shrugged. "That was Frankenstein's helper's name."

"But he was a hunchback," I said, not quite comprehending the connection.

"Maybe," Ben drawled out, "maybe it's because I frequently feel like Dr. Frankenstein."

I watched him place Igor, still on the pen, inside his pocket again. A cold, emotionless smile crossed Ben's face as he stood up and crossed to the doorway. He opened it slowly, with exaggerated deliberation. "Shall we be on our way? My dungeon at El Fin del Camino has many hungry creatures waiting for their dinner."

Passing before him to reach the hallway, I was overwhelmingly grateful to Tharon Ann for calling when she did. Someone knew I was still alive on this date, and where I was going, and how I could be reached. Someone knew there was a Ben, a nephew. It suddenly seemed terribly important to me. Not just the comfort of a friend knowing where I was . . . but more vitally, that Ben knew I had a friend in the world, someone who would care, who would worry if I wasn't heard from. I suddenly remembered Ben's offer to let me watch one of his snakes eat a live rat—and I couldn't help wondering if snakes ate people too. It was an image too gruesome to dwell upon. . . .

✻✧✻

The wind howled outside the dining-room windows, whisking a light snowfall into swirling apparitions in the darkness beyond, as Melanie brought in the coffee and a freshly baked apple cake on a tray. Ben had long since absented himself to retreat to his cellarful of deadly pets.

"Well," William Musser said, leaning back in the heavy oak chair while he lighted a panetella. "I think it's a crazy scheme. How do you propose to coerce either Prescott or Melendez into being taken with Alyce?"

William turned and smiled at me in a gesture that indicated he hadn't said it to imply I was unattractive. I had not taken offense, and I smiled back at him to indicate it. Of all the Musser family, William struck me as the most well-integrated personality. He had a wiry frame, the kind of physique that announces an active person. About fifty-two or -three, he didn't have the saturated tan that Alexander and Mansfield Watersdown displayed, and so many other faces I had already encountered in that remote area of California. While there was a healthy tautness to his skin, it was plain that he spent more time inside the borax mine than out working the ranch.

William's hair was salt-and-pepper gray, short and bordering on kinky; his eyebrows were like a fox terrier's, bushy and also on the kinky side. He had a very broad smile, which he used comparatively often, a short forehead, and a straight, narrow nose. Seated next to Alexander, he seemed a very direct person, devoid of pomposity or airs. I had liked him the moment we met just before sitting down to dinner, and his presence had made me feel infinitely better about being in Frazier. Other than Manny, William seemed the only person I could feel at ease with; while I didn't dislike Alex or Melanie, I didn't feel totally comfortable about them or around them. Of course, I attributed this to my basic shyness around new people or situations, but I was terribly pleased that William would be around. It rather mitigated Ben and his cellar. After all, El Fin del Camino was a very, very long distance away from any other home or family. With Ben around, I felt like a prisoner; with Alex, more like a guest. Melanie was unfathomable. Her world was the room she was in; her mind drifted with fragments of conversation, sometimes appropriately, sometimes not.

But William seemed solid, dependable. He made me feel like family—distant only insofar as we'd not met before, but respectful of the blood relationship.

". . . And as I said, we've really got nothing to lose," Alex was saying, bringing my thoughts back to the topic.

"How do you propose to arrange a meeting?" William asked. "Something subtle, like a debut ball?" He puffed on his cigar, sending blue smoke to hover beneath the chandelier.

"Don't be difficult, William," Alex growled. "We can begin with Juan Melendez. He's a veterinarian. We have horses and livestock on the ranch. What could be more natural than to ask him to come by to see Fury?"

"Is Fury not feeling well?" Melanie asked, pouring the last cup of coffee and taking her place across from Alexander. "She's my favorite, dear," Melanie turned to me and said. "A wonderful roan, just as gentle as a horse can be."

"Of course she is," Alexander replied, his eyebrows raising with forced patience. "We simply have to *say* that Fury has been off his feed. Then Juan will come by to take a look at him, and we'll introduce Juan to Alyce."

"I hear folks saying that Juan's been spending a lot of time up in Bakersfield. Strikes me he may well have a girl friend up there. What would that do to your carefully laid plans!"

Alexander *tsked* irritably. "What unmarried man doesn't have a girl friend, William! That doesn't mean he's necessarily serious about her."

William pondered on this for a few moments, glancing from Alex to me as if weighing the odds of the plan. "I grant you," he began slowly, "Alyce is the best-looking woman around these parts. Maybe you're right. Maybe Juan would prefer to avoid the long drive just for some female companionship."

"Aren't there any young women in Frazier?" I asked. After all, at thirty I could hardly be considered a wisp of a girl, bound to catch every man's eye.

"None that an educated and wealthy man would care to spend an evening with in *social* intercourse, if you get my meaning," William answered. "Juan's not the type to waste his time," he added.

Alex sipped his coffee slowly, almost rolling it in his mouth like a fine wine. "Excellent coffee, Melanie, as always. There's not a woman alive who makes better coffee than you do."

Melanie flushed with pleasure, and busied herself with slicing the apple cake into perfect wedges. I marveled at her deftness; had I done it, the cake would have looked like hamburger. Whatever her emotional or mental problems might be, Melanie was brilliant in the kitchen. Her talents in that direction were easily understood; it was the first time I had heard anyone compliment her about anything. It was her domain, and she took pride in excelling at it. Obviously, Melanie lived in order to care for her brothers and nephew; she seemed to have no other motivation or interest of any consequence.

"Then how do we work in Kyle Prescott?" William asked, accepting the plain white plate from Melanie and passing it along to Alexander.

I had half expected that Alex would then pass it along to me, not only as a female guest at his table, but out of ordinary courtesy to any newcomer in his home. He didn't, however, and the act triggered my remembering the way he had served himself sherry earlier in the day, not thinking to serve anyone else until his glass was poured. It was a small giveaway, and

not terribly important, but it was definitely an indication of
his self-image.

"Kyle presents something of a problem," Alex conceded.

"Kyle has a gold mine," Melanie told me enthusiastically.

"Yes," Alex interrupted. "Alyce's gold mine . . . *our* mine."

"And what about you, Alyce," William said. "Assuming you
can find any papers or letters which would incriminate either
of the fathers of these two, what then? Why should you share
it with us? We're only half kin to you, and no relation at all to
your father's interests in that fortune."

I faltered for a moment, distracted briefly by Melanie's slow
finger-drumming on the table. She seemed to be picking out a
tune at an invisible piano, then unexpectedly looked up at me
and her round blue eyes rested on me. She let the corners of
her mouth twist up in secrecy, and placed her hand in her lap.

Alex had leaned forward for my reply, his doleful amber
eyes impatient for my answer. I wrapped both hands around
the steaming cup of coffee, and prayed for lucid thoughts to
flow. "I've never wanted great wealth, William. Never cared
about it. But being cheated out of it, knowing the hardships it
caused our mother—well, then I do care. Not for the value so
much, but for, for . . ."

"Surely not revenge," Melanie said slowly.

Her mind wasn't so far away after all, obviously. "No. Not
that. Justice, I guess. Torn from her children, forced from her
home and her friends. Having to go live in anonymity, in poverty . . . in fear. No. Not revenge, justice."

"But why share it with us?" William persisted.

I had to smile at his question. My feelings were very
difficult to express, yet as inarticulate as they were, I knew in
my heart what I wanted to convey. "You three have paid for
this fortune much more than I have. If my father had died a
natural death, Mother would have stayed on in Frazier, have
remained close to her three children . . . and to me. I was too
young to feel any loss, and too ignorant of the events to actually suffer as a result of my father's murder."

"That's really quite true, you know," Alex said softly, leaning back in his chair with blatant relief.

"It seems to me," I resumed, "that if we can recover any of
this stolen fortune, it would be my moral obligation to share it

with all of you. Mother wouldn't have had it any other way—had circumstances turned out otherwise."

"A fine woman," Melanie added, slicing another piece of cake, for me this time. "You're very much like her, dear. Very much."

William sent a blue-gray vapor of smoke over our heads. "Well, then we're in accord about the proceeds, but not about the methods. We still have to figure how to get Kyle Prescott around here."

"A party!" Melanie exclaimed. "Let's have a party! Could we? Oh, please, couldn't we have a party?"

Alex thumped his large, gnarled hand on the white table-cloth. "That's it! Of course! That's the perfect solution!"

"How're you going to pay for it, Alex? We can't afford a big do and you know it."

"We could make it a picnic," Melanie said. "A country-style picnic, with everyone bringing something."

"Wouldn't have to serve any hard liquor that way," Alex added.

"You won't get Kyle here without the promise of liquor," William pointed out.

"Then, dammit," Alex roared, "he can bring his own. Let the liquor be his contribution. God knows, *he* can damned well afford it!"

A short silence ensued as the idea grew on all of us. It seemed perfectly logical, and the simplest possible means for me to meet the two men without arousing suspicions. No need for deceit or pretense, just an old-fashioned social do.

Fury's off her feed, indeed! I thought.

CHAPTER NINE

After clearing off the dining table, the men went off to go over the accounts receivable and payable aspects of running a ranch and a small mine. It didn't surprise me that neither of them had made any offer to help Melanie and me in the cleaning up. In their remote, microcosmic world, a woman still belonged in the kitchen while men took care of the "important" things. It didn't seem to bother Melanie, and as long as I wouldn't have to live with it for the rest of my life, I didn't really care. Besides, it gave me an opportunity to get to know Melanie better.

The kitchen was enormous, larger than most farmhouses would boast. There was an inactive Franklin stove right next to an old, but serviceable, gas stove. When I asked why they had both, Melanie giggled and explained that none of them really trusted the more modern conveniences. "And too," she added, "when you live in the wilds, there's many a time when pipes freeze. Or the roads are so iced that we can't get our butane shipment on time. Nice to have the dependable reserve of a wood-burning stove on hand."

She methodically washed each dish, scraping at any hint of food particle with her short fingernails till she was satisfied the plate was sparkling clean. I wiped them, mindful to get them as bone dry as my mother would have insisted upon; in my own apartment, I never bothered to dry dishes. "I suppose, then, that the energy crisis doesn't worry you too much."

Melanie paused, suds dripping from her plump hands. "Crisis?"

I smiled, though I'm not sure if it was to take the onus off the term so much as shock that she was unaware of a crisis. "Yes, the shortages of oil and gas. Weren't you affected by it in recent winters?"

She returned my smile as if I were talking about life on a polar cap. "Well, dear, I wouldn't know about such things. I'm certain that if there's a shortage of anything, Alexander will take care of it somehow. He's most resourceful, you know."

From the kitchen window, and even in the pitch darkness of the night, there was sufficient light from the house itself to make out the fringe of trees beyond the yard. "Well, of course, you could always chop down trees for heat."

"Heaven forbid, child! We're not permitted to touch the trees around here—not a one! This is a national forest, Alyce. Nothing gets cut down without the government's permission. Then, too, there're the birds to worry about."

"Birds?"

"My yes! Just over the next range, there's one of the world's largest condor preserves, not to mention all sorts of other wild birds and creatures. Not many people know about Frazier National Park, but those of us who live here are terribly proud of it. Why, Alexander would rather see a plague strike every human in this area than to see one tree felled. He's really most adamant about it. . . ."

Her voice held such forceful conviction that it took me aback somewhat. Then I remembered Manny's statement about Alexander being involved in litigation over the house. "Is that part of the Spanish land-grant problem over this ranch?"

She shrugged. "I know little about such things, Alyce. But the government, as I understand it, says that we have no right to own land in the middle of a national preserve; that we can lease it, but we can't own it. You'd best ask Alexander if you want a clearer idea about it all."

I was quiet for a few moments, letting Melanie return to her usual calm and optimism. My questions had unsettled her, and since I was leading up to more important ones, I wanted her to feel at ease before I broached them. We finished the dishes, and I took the large shopping sack filled with garbage out to the tin garbage pail just outside on the back porch. When I re-entered, Melanie was pouring herself another cup of coffee.

"Would you like some?" she asked sweetly.

I didn't, really, but felt it might offend her if I refused. So I nodded yes, and we sat down at the round oak table in the kitchen. She'd thoughtfully found an ashtray from somewhere and had placed it near me. It had come from a hotel or a casino at some point in time, but was so old the lettering was no longer discernible. We remained in comfortable silence for a few moments, and I could tell that this was probably Melanie's favorite time of day; the work is done, the household quiet; and I was certain that everyone would retire soon. Even a city girl knows that people who work the land get up with the sun; and as their guest, I expected I would do the same, though it would probably take a few days for my system to get used to it.

"You know, Alyce, I was twenty when Mamma moved away." She laughed deprecatingly. "My, I thought I was all so grown-up then! I was betrothed to a handsome young man with a wonderful kindness about him, and everything was going to be beautiful forevermore! Looking back on it now, I was just a child. Land sakes, how we do deceive ourselves when we are young!"

I knew perfectly what she meant, and could readily empathize. But more importantly, she herself had brought up the topic I'd been anxious to question her about. "How did it all happen, Melanie—if you don't mind my asking."

She tilted her head quizzically, her mind in obvious pursuit to re-create the era, the tempo of so long ago. "I can still see it all," she began slowly, "just like in a movie. None of us begrudged Mamma remarryin'. She was still so full of life, so vibrant, we were old enough to understand that she needed companionship. She married Mr. Laird in, let's see, about late '43 or early '44; I remember the war was still raging, but I don't exactly recall the precise date of their wedding. Mr. Laird was a nice enough man, and while he wasn't wealthy, we all knew that the gold mine he worked would soon begin to pay off. The assayers were most optimistic about the mine, and we all knew it was just a matter of hitting the mother lode. Mr. Laird was a *very* hard worker."

"Were you living with him, then?" I asked cautiously, not wanting to trip Melanie back into her own private world.

"I was, of course. Proper young ladies didn't leave home 'til they were married. Leastways, not around here, they didn't. And William, too. He was just a teen-ager and still going to high school." She paused, her eyes twinkling with mirth. "You might not believe this, but we still have the same old two-story schoolhouse—it houses the entire educational benefits for miles and miles around, from kindergarten right on up to the twelfth grade. Principal and his Mrs. live upstairs, just as it's always been since the school was built in '20. But I'm wandering, dear, forgive me. You were askin'?"

"About living with my father."

"Oh yes! As I said, two of us were living on the kindness of your father. Alexander, though, had decided to strike off on his own. He was nigh on to twenty-three, as I recall, and didn't much like the idea of living with a stepfather. Besides, he was already courting Beth then, and it looked pretty certain they'd be tying the knot soon. Because our father had owned a borax mine and land—though not nearly as big as this hacienda—Alexander got Mamma's permission to sell it to the bank as a down payment on this spread. The land was fertile, and Alexander has always been good with the land. It's good artichoke farming around here, and good grazing land for the stock."

"It certainly didn't look like it when I first drove up," I said in surprise, remembering the arid barrenness of the area where Manny lived.

"Oh, my dear, that's over the hill you're talking about! The moment you get into the forest, it's an entirely different world! If you're here when the snow thaws, you'll see what I mean."

"Then, Alexander bought this place and married. . . ."

"Beth. Nice enough girl. Little snooty for my tastes. But I reasoned that so was Alexander, so it was probably a good match." She laughed at her own comment. "Alexander is a good man, Alyce, but he *does* take some gettin' to know. First-born sons seem to be more aggressive, don't you think?"

"I'd never thought about it," I confessed.

"Well, that's my thinking about it. Alexander and Beth moved in here as soon as they were married, and we didn't see as much of them as I would have liked. But life was comfortable enough at your father's house, and at least we still had Mamma. And, as I said, I was planning to marry soon myself."

"Did you always call my father Mr. Laird?" I asked lightly.

Melanie pursed her lips in amusement. "Well, we were too old to call him Papa, and he didn't like being called Mr. Laird. Mamma wouldn't let us call him Horatio—and besides, William and I would just go into giggling fits whenever his first name was used. Most the time, I guess, we just called him Sir. He suggested Uncle, but it just didn't seem right. Alexander called him Horatio, but then, he was older and it seemed more fittin'."

"And my father's partners, were they socially close too? I mean, did they all socialize together or was it strictly a business arrangement?"

She laughed heartily. "Honey, this is Frazier, not Boston! If you don't socialize with everyone around, you'd end up seeing no one at all! We don't have very many people living around here. Oh, there are the people who drive in with their campers and the like, but they're just tourists and we wouldn't call on strangers! But the folks who live in Frazier have a feeling of kindredship about each other, like we're all part of a grand family. There are squabbles, of course, and times when this one isn't talking to that one, but it all passes. We stick together, for the most part. So, of course, Mr. Prescott and Mr. Melendez were frequent visitors to your father's house."

"I'd always thought there was some prejudice against the Mexicans in the Southwest," I said, thinking of the farm labor problems and the illegal aliens we read about in Boston.

"Over in Salinas, yes. I even hear that Los Angeles is terribly prejudiced toward them. But here in Frazier it's different. The few Mexicans left around here are of the monied classes, of Spanish ancestry. If it hadn't been for the Mexicans, there probably wouldn't be a Frazier at all. They settled it, and they defended it shoulder-to-shoulder against attack or with our boys during the Civil War."

"I didn't think the Civil War reached California," I said, amazed at the information, and strongly doubting it.

Melanie drummed chubby fingers on the tabletop, her forehead furrowed in an apparent attempt to recall her history. "We weren't part of the Union yet, but we had cattle and food, and we had gold. Both sides were mighty interested in helping themselves to our resources. We had already declared ourselves a free territory, rejecting the concept of slavery, so of course most settlers were in sympathy with the Union. But a lot of Californians volunteered to fight for the Confederate side in that conflict. You must run up and visit Fort Tejon while you're here, it's a marvelously preserved fort, and an historical landmark."

She was veering again, though I knew it was my own fault, so I tried to break her trend of thought by pouring us both some more coffee. "So eyebrows weren't raised if Mexicans were entertained socially. . . ."

"Heavens no! Not around here, they weren't. Old Carlos Melendez was quite a prominent man in these parts! As I recall, he even ran for the alderman's office, or something like that—almost won, too! I think, Alyce, that you've got a picture of peons in your head—broad sombreros, brightly colored serapes, and all that. Why, girl, those are the poor people, the illiterate laborers. They have nothing in common with the upper-class Mexicans. Just you wait till you meet Juan! Now there's a man to turn *any* girl's head!"

"And Kyle Prescott?" I asked.

She shook her head as if I'd asked a stupid question. "You can't compare one to the other; it's a question of personal preference. Kyle's a blond, blue-eyed type. As different from each other as grits are to ham! There's no saying one's better, they're just different."

William strolled in at that moment, a serious expression on his face as if he were trying to retain an equation in his mind. "Girls getting to know each other?" he asked absently as he poured himself a cup of coffee.

"We surely are, William," Melanie replied cheerfully. "It's so *nice* to have another lady to talk to after supper!"

He smiled beatifically at Melanie, then at me. "I'm very

happy to hear that," he said. "Now, don't stay up too late, you promise?"

"I promise, William," Melanie answered seriously.

He kissed the top of her gray head, nodded toward me, and left the kitchen with cup in hand. There was a moment's lull after he'd departed, and I was desperately holding myself in rein lest I bombard Melanie with questions too soon. After a bit, I lighted a cigarette.

"Surprised Mamma let you smoke," Melanie stated casually.

I laughed. "She didn't approve, you can be sure of that."

"Shouldn't have thought so. But ladies nowadays do pretty much as they please, don't they."

"The lucky ones do," I replied. Then, before we got too far afield, I asked, "How did my father die, Melanie?"

She frowned, her blue eyes darkening to almost a slate hue. "It wasn't a nice way to go," she said. "Somebody blew his head off with a double-barrel shotgun."

I shuddered at the image. "But there's no way that could possibly have been considered an 'accident,'" I exploded, then tried to bring myself under control again.

"Well, they did. It was your father's own gun that killed him. They said it was suicide."

"On what basis? Did he have any reason to kill himself?"

"None that we knew of. Oh, he was having a lot of trouble with his partners, and it seemed they were always arguing about something toward the end. But at home, he was always cordial and just doted on Mamma. It didn't seem likely he'd blow his brains out."

"But the partners made it look that way?"

"There was no proving it," Melanie replied. "But you should talk to Alexander about that, or even William. I was so in love with Mitchell at that time, I wasn't paying very close attention to your father's mining interests."

Somehow I had the prudence not to pursue the subject of Melanie's dead fiancé; I could see the pain in her eyes when she mentioned his name.

"I think it's time we turned in," Melanie suggested after a brief silence. "I'll show you to your room."

We rose, turned off the kitchen lights, and I followed her toward the back of the house where a narrow stairway led to the second floor. "It's a very nice room, Alyce," Melanie said, leading the way up the stairs. "Wallpaper's a little faded now, but it gets the sun all day long and has a nice view of Mount Pinos. I reckon the skiers will all be coming up now, what with the snowfall and all," she sighed as we reached the landing.

Melanie pointed to the doorway on the right, saying it was her bedroom. On the left, directly across from hers, was my room. The doors to both rooms were ajar. As we entered, I could see my luggage neatly stacked in one corner, out of the way. But it was a corner room, with windows on two sides. The decor was nothing exceptional, just durable. However, what made all the difference in the world was a small fireplace, and someone had been kind enough to build a fire, which threw cozy shadows and warmth across the furniture and the walls. Such a luxury really delighted me, and especially with the snow gently collecting upon the window panes. The wind had died down, and I felt as if I'd entered a storybook world.

Melanie crossed to the fireplace and stoked it efficiently. "Glad Ben remembered to light it, he's such a forgetful lad sometimes." She turned, surveying the area carefully, and satisfied with what she saw, she walked toward me and placed a chubby hand on my arm. "I'm so glad you're staying with us, Alyce. We'll talk again . . . soon."

She placed a light kiss on my cheek, and with a brief "God bless" left the room, closing the door softly behind her. Glancing at my watch, I saw that it wasn't even nine o'clock yet, and I smiled to myself. While I was emotionally tired from the long, arduous day, inclusive of the drive to and from Los Angeles and Ben's peculiar personality, it was still not likely that I could just climb into bed and go to sleep at once. I decided to unpack my clothes instead. I'd just begun, my suitcases open atop the bed, when I heard a piercing scream.

It sounded very much like Melanie, and I dropped my dress to the floor as I raced for the bedroom door. Even as I reached Melanie's door, I could hear the heavy footfalls of men running up the stairs at the far end of the landing. I rapped on her door loudly, calling Melanie's name. When there was no reply, I rudely barged into the room.

She lay on the worn carpet, breathing heavily, moaning softly to herself. "Stay back, Alyce! Don't come in here!"

"But Melanie!" I protested, noticing a swelling begin to bloat her calf. "What in God's name . . ."

"Just stay back! It's still in here somewhere!"

"*What*'s still in here?"

Just as Alexander and William reached the doorway, I saw it. It was sort of a grayish-brown, the body a pulpy two inches across and covered with hair. Its ten hairy legs were like sluggish tendrils, each about six inches in length. I couldn't stifle the scream that formed in my throat as it waddled across the floor.

"Where'd that tarantula come from?" Alexander demanded.

"Forget that," William countered. "Let's get Doc Adams over here right away!"

I was so terrified with that creature loose in the room that I was literally rooted to the floor, unable to assist the two men as they gently lifted Melanie and placed her on the bed. All I could do was stare at that hairy thing in a horror so enormous I felt nauseated at the sight, yet I was unable to pull my eyes away from it.

"I'll call the doctor," Alexander said, leaving the room as if I weren't present. Wasn't anyone going to catch the thing? Throw it away? Put it outside? Do *something!* My mind screamed at me to see if I could be of comfort to Melanie, but my limbs wouldn't obey while the creature was in my view.

"Alyce, snap out of it," William commanded.

With a wrenching effort, my gaze turned in the direction of his voice. He was examining the bite on Melanie's calf, squeezing it in an attempt to get the venom out. But I was still frozen to the floor.

"Alyce!" he ordered again.

Melanie lay perspiring on the bed, a seizure of shaking in her bones, though from the bite itself or out-and-out terror, I didn't know. My mind was in turmoil. I couldn't move, nor speak. I wanted to point to the tarantula, to demand that it be taken away or killed . . . but I couldn't. I didn't even see William leave the bedside as my own terror mounted and mounted. Not till the slap of his hand snapped my head to one side did I come out of the stupor of fear.

I was still afraid, but William had done the right thing. His slap had shaken my state of shock, and I began to come back to the reality of the moment, of Melanie's need—not just my own recoiling horror. And just at that moment, Alexander returned to the room, saying that Dr. Adams was on his way. He had with him a shoe box, and it was with an overwhelming sense of relief that I saw him place it directly on top of the spider. "Damn that Ben," he muttered. "I'll skin that boy alive if this is one of his infernal creatures!"

The shoe box moved slightly as the tarantula tried to escape its confines. I felt my knees turn to jelly, and if it hadn't been for William's stern glance, I probably would have fainted.

"Of course it's one of Ben's," William replied, his hand stroking Melanie's forehead as she lay there, eyes wide with fright and confusion. "The question isn't one of ownership, but how the hell it got into this room!"

❖

After the doctor had left, I returned to my room in a state of turmoil, fear, anxiety, and bone-chilling fear. Despite the fact that I'd been assured the bite from a tarantula is not lethal (unless one had some allergy or weakened condition), the image of that horrible, hairy creature couldn't be erased from my mind.

Dr. Adams had made a very small incision where the bite had occurred, forced as much blood as possible from the wound, and then applied a paste made up of baking soda and calamine lotion, with a very small amount of menthol. He placed a small gauze pad over the area to make sure the paste wouldn't rub off during the night, acknowledged my presence with a perfunctory noncurious nod, and left the house as quickly as he'd arrived. Under other circumstances, I might well have requested some sort of sedative to see me through the night, but I was embarrassed to appear such an emotional child.

Ben had been summoned, naturally, and, wearing a heavy leather glove, he'd lifted the box off the spider carefully, then instantly clamped a rather large clear plastic box over the insect, gradually slipping a mesh-topped lid beneath it until the hairy thing was tightly enclosed in its terrarium. It seemed to rear up on its back legs for a few moments, and the underside of its legs had what looked like pads of iridescent hairs.

Apparently, neither William nor Alex felt it was the proper time to scold Ben about the wanderings of his pet. He left the room without a word, and William suggested that I had best go to bed and try to forget the unfortunate incident. He had no idea of just how "unfortunate" it was for me; as a city girl, I felt as if my blood had stopped flowing in my veins.

Lying in the comfortable bed, I tried desperately to sleep—but couldn't. Every strange sound, every rustling leaf against a window pane, brought the vivid memory of that thing thumping against the shoe box back to mind. I couldn't shake the awful fear that there was something under the covers at the foot of my bed, that there were other "escaped" tarantulas slowly climbing up the bedspread. I couldn't stop shuddering, my flesh literally crawling with revulsion and fear. If I changed position, even slightly, and the bedsheet happened to graze my ankle, I gasped involuntarily—imagining some insect lurking beneath the covers, about to spring at me. In absolute exasperation with myself, yet unable to master my fear, I turned the bedside light on and threw the covers back. All the way. There was nothing in my bed. Nothing at all. Then, mustering all the courage I could, I lifted the lamp down to the floor, where I got on my hands and knees and carefully scanned beneath the bed. Nothing.

Satisfied that my emotions were out of control and my fears mere childish fantasies, I climbed back into the bed and again turned off the light. I closed my eyes, determined to go to sleep. A distant rustling sound brought me bolt upright in the bed, my pulse points pounding throughout my body.

Silly as it was, feeling every bit like a child who'd just seen a horror movie, I again turned on the bedside lamp. I didn't care what anyone might think about me, I was scared out of my wits—and if sleep came at all, I would at least know the light was on.

When I awakened in the morning, the lamp was still on; a feeble illumination amidst the snow-reflected sunlight that filled my bedroom like a solar prominence.

CHAPTER TEN

The next few days were spent in relative quiet. Once the shock of the spider bite had passed, Melanie was right back to her cheerful, fey self, bustling with plans for the country-style picnic everyone had agreed to. Alex was out of the house first, with a reluctant and grumbling Ben foot-dragging behind him, to oversee the farmhands and seeing to it that their few head of cattle were being properly taken care of now that the snow had packed itself solidly across the grazing areas. William would leave about an hour later, off to work the borax mine.

Once the final guest list had been written up, discussed, and approved by Alex, there next came the task of writing out the invitations. This task fell very largely to me as the most expendable member in the household. And because Melanie had already set about baking spice and fruit cakes, which she would subsequently wrap in heavy aluminum foil and then ask Ben to larder in the cellar, I elected to write up the invitations at the kitchen table. At least we could chat, and if there were any questions about the spelling of a name, or the street address, she was right there to answer them. It seemed that they knew people from all over the area: people in Gorman, Lebec, Grapevine, Lake of the Woods, Piñon Pines, Cuddy Valley, on and on. Strange names to my Boston ears. And, naturally, invitations had to be sent to the pastor of El Camino Pines Chapel—"They're Lutherans," Melanie explained, "but very fine folk"—and the Seventh-Day Adventists, the Assembly of God, and other denominations; the availability of religious worship was amazing to me in view of the remoteness of the area and the small population.

I also became familiar with their local newspaper, *The Mountain Enterprise,* and felt like a shifty city slicker as I read lead articles about the local Girl Scout chapter, someone in the hospital with a possible heart attack, the VFW barbecue on the front page, not to mention the Fiesta Days Whiskerino Contest—obviously to see which man could grow the best beard. It was so terribly woodsy and folksy that I began really to look forward to the winter picnic, forgetting momentarily the underlying reason for it in the first place. How a murder could have occurred in this atmosphere baffled me completely.

So for two days, while the torturously salivating aromas of Melanie's cakes pervaded the house all day, I wrote out more than 125 invitations to an old-fashioned everybody-bring-something picnic. Children welcome. Anyone willing and able to play a guitar, banjo, or fiddle could have all the food and beer he wanted for free—but he'd have to earn it, because there'd be a hoedown as soon as the sun set. Due to the heavy snowfall, it would be held in the barn. The makeshift tables would be moved out of the way for the dancing; and if anyone wanted to, they could go on a sleigh hayride later on. Ladies were to wear long dresses, but men could come as they liked. There'd be punch for the teetotalers, and anyone desiring hard spirits had best bring their own.

I simply could not believe I was living through the entire preparation, and found myself unable to imagine the event itself. I speculated if men would have to check their guns at the door, or where the sulkies and wagons would be hitched. It was so totally alien to anything I'd ever experienced, I began to feel as if I were living in a Hollywood movie—except that this was not at all make-believe, it was quite serious and obviously the main means of entertainment for people in Frazier. Yet Melanie's excitement shattered any pseudo-sophisticated veneer that may have lurked in my Bostonian heart; she was infectious with light-hearted and busy preparations. The picnic had been set for the following weekend, and there was a good deal to be accomplished. Bread had to be baked, hams readied, potato salad and garbanzo beans marinated; the woman was amazing!

"Now then, Alyce, don't you worry about there not being enough food for all those people," she said toward the end of the third day. "There'll be beef and pork, the Gomezes always bring enough *frijoles* to choke the nation, and then señora Gomez always makes up her homemade tamales—and they're somethin' to write home about, let me tell you! Clara Schmidt always brings her mamma's German cole slaw, and Etta Morris makes candied yams that leave a body rollin' on the ground from wanting more. It's goin' to be a mighty fine occasion, Alyce, you mark my words!"

"It sounds like a United Nations convention." I laughed.

She wiped her hands on her apron, nodding significantly. "You'll see," she said, then surveyed the kitchen to be sure it was all tidied. "You planning on helping me clean house, or are you just going to sit on your caboose all day!"

I laughed at her pretended sternness. "I'm at your disposal, Melanie. Just tell me what you want done."

"Dust mop's in the porch, clean dustcloths are in the hamper next to it. You get started with the floors and the dustin', and I'll see to the vacuuming—it's an old machine and needs knowin' how to use it. Then we'll set about washing all the bric-a-brac—you're a good, willin' worker, Alyce, that's plain to see."

My effort to curtsy was a little awkward, but I managed to raise a smile out of Melanie. "It's because we had the same mamma," I answered.

❁

By Thursday, the house gleamed. Everyone had phoned with their acceptances or their reasons for being unable to attend; we would be a party of 107—including, we were all smugly satisfied to note, one Kyle Prescott and one Juan Melendez. Once that was firmly established, I found myself on a teeter-totter of contradicting emotions. I looked forward to this western picnic and hoedown as I'd never looked forward to anything in my life; I was terrified at the prospect of meeting Mssrs. Prescott and Melendez.

But no matter how I tried to soothe my emotions, how hard

I struggled to put things into a calmer, more sophisticated perspective . . . I was excited, elated, scared, worried, and about as blasé as a seven-year-old on Christmas Eve.

✳❖✳

"Do-se-do and allemande left!"

The nasal command, given in a singsong tone in tempo with the strident violin and metallic banjo accompaniment, was a no-nonsense, toe-tapping, knee-slapping, guaranteed-to-cure-what-ails-you instruction to the twenty or more couples square-dancing on the dirt floor of the huge barn. Actually, there were two fiddles, one banjo, and one guitar, and the noise reverberated from the rafters. The barn was filled with music and laughter as couples clasped hands in an unending chain of switching partners within the circle. The ladies, in their long gowns, dressed to the nines for the occasion, presented a colorful, swirling picture; while the men, dressed mostly in jeans and checkered shirts—some were even wearing cowboy boots—looked their Sunday-best, with cowlicks smoothed in place, and closely shaven, rugged faces. I'd not danced as yet because I'd been too busy helping Melanie and señora Gomez clearing off some of the tables with the more perishable foods, and taking them back to the kitchen inside the house. I don't know what I'd expected from señora Mary Gomez, but she looked about as Mexican as Mary Tyler Moore. Her husband was a forest ranger, and if either of them fitted the stereotyped picture of "Chicanos," then I was an Arab. They were both brunettes, yes; but, obviously, there was no hint of Indian blood in their faces.

I liked Mary instantly. She was in her late twenties, attending college part-time in Fresno, working toward her master's degree in cultural anthropology, and planned to devote much of her time—once her degree was conferred—to working with the itinerate Mexican laborers around Fresno, helping them to assimilate into North American society. "It'll have to be as a volunteer," she said with a small shrug of her slender shoulders while wrapping up the leftover hams in Saran Wrap. "I don't want to get all locked into the bureaucracy by becoming a social worker. These laborers don't need social workers, they need to be educated about their heritage, taught to be proud of themselves—regardless of what kind of work they do."

"But won't they be going back to Mexico?" Melanie asked, munching happily on a cold tamale.

"Some will," Mary conceded. "But most of them will travel with the seasons to work with whatever crops need tending at that time. Most of them live on next to nothing, saving their meager earnings so they can someday send for their families."

"If they leave their families behind," I asked naïvely, "how do their wives and children manage to survive?" I gestured to Melanie to hand me a few plastic containers for the leftover cole slaw, the strains of the hoedown filtering in across the bitterly cold night.

"Some send money across the border. But usually the wives get jobs as domestics or salesclerks."

"Well, they're obviously not interested in welfare or unemployment programs," I said with a growing admiration for these people.

Mary laughed heartily. "You've got to be joking! The average Chicano is fiercely proud . . . it's your *gringos* who have grown up to expect the government to support them."

"But I don't understand," I began as Melanie clamped the lids on the plastic containers. "Just what is a Chicano? I mean, are you one?"

"*Quién? Yo?* Chure, lathy!" Mary replied with a faked, heavy accent. "The joke's on everyone, in my book. Allegedly, the term is only applied to the peons, or the obvious Indian-Mexican. But that's not the way it's defined by the Establishment. They don't specify that one has to be of Indian blood; they just say a Chicano is anyone of Mexican parents who was born in this country. So I fit—right?"

"But why," Melanie chirped, "then, does everyone assume that all Mexicans are lower-class laborers, all dark and swarthy?"

Mary lifted her hands, then brought them down to her thighs with a light slap. "Why does everyone think all Scandinavians are blonds? Ignorance, Melanie. Sheer ignorance—and a need to peg people in cubbyholes. All Jews are shrewd in business, all blacks got rhythm, all Italians are opera singers . . . shall I go on?"

"No, please don't." I laughed.

Melanie rolled up a loaf of bread in a dampened cloth and put it in the refrigerator. "I went to school with an Italian girl," she mused. "She couldn't even sing 'Jingle Bells' in tune."

"Speaking of," Mary said, surveying the kitchen for any additional leftovers, "what do you think of Juan Melendez?"

"He seems very nice," I hedged. Actually, my reaction to him earlier in the evening had been very mixed. While he was polite, courteously welcoming me to Frazier, he seemed remote, even secretive. Granted, he was an exceptionally handsome man—in an unusual sort of way. A little more than six feet tall, he was lean, with a tennis player's physique. His eyes were a dark brown, guarded, and tilted slightly upward beneath thick black eyebrows. His handshake had been firm, and I noted that he had exceptionally attractive hands for a man—more like a sculptor's or what one imagines a musician's hands should be like, with a broad palm and long, strong, tapering fingers. There was something about Juan Melendez that made me feel he should be dipped in bronze and placed in front of the public library or the town square. Yet there was an arrogance about him that left an unpleasant impression upon me. But then, I reminded myself, we'd only exchanged how-do-you-do's and I was being grossly unfair.

"He's very formal 'til he gets to know you," Mary said, breaking into my thoughts. "He's also a conscientious vet, even though he doesn't have to do anything for a living."

No, I thought, of course he doesn't; he's living off my money—and then instantly chastised myself for such a churlish and unproven opinion. "Shall we go back to the dance?" I suggested.

"Melanie? You going to stay in the kitchen all night long?"

"No, no, Mary. You two go on along, I'll be there in a moment. I just want to put some of these things away, and throw out the rest of this trash in the garbage pail."

"I can do that," I said, not wanting poor Melanie to be stuck with all the dirty work.

"Now, don't you fret, Alyce! Go have a good time! After all, the party's in your honor . . . 'sides, I may just lie down for a few moments, I'm feeling just a little tuckered out."

Mary and I exchanged knowing glances. "Then you march straight upstairs, Melanie," she said authoritatively, "and I'll take care of that. And you, Alyce, you go on back to the party. I'll be out shortly."

There was absolutely no room in her attitude for argument, so I smiled, took one of Melanie's shawls off the peg, and went through the dining room to the double doors that led to the courtyard between the house and the barn. Crunching contentedly across the packed snow, the music and happy chatting and laughter drifting across the sharp, biting air like leaves on a pond, I marveled at the difference in life-styles between the East and the West. Yet, I supposed, farmers in Massachusetts also had hoedowns. I'd never thought about it before, and made a mental note to learn more about my home state when I returned. There's something about city life that seems to exclude, almost mock, any other form of life. It then seemed a self-defeating exclusion: the quasi-sophisticates disdaining the rural without any true knowledge of it.

"Swing with your partner and skip to M'lou . . ."

I stood at the open barn door and just watched for a few moments. Despite the piercing cold out of doors, obviously the dancers were warm and required the fresh air to circulate through the huge area. I could dimly make out a young couple up in the hayloft, and hoped that no one else could see them —especially their parents. The kerosene lanterns sent mischievous shadows throughout the barn, and there was a blanket of warmth at the sight of these good people, neighbors, friends, husbands and wives, children scampering or imitating their dancing parents—people who, for the occasion, hadn't a care in the world. The very earth trembled in time with the music and the dancing couples, and I fantasized that even the worms and underground insects were holding small parties of their own.

"You've not danced yet."

The baritone voice startled me completely, and I whirled to see Juan Melendez standing behind me. His knit brows and slight smile indicated an apology for having caught me by surprise. "No one's asked me," I replied simply. "Besides, I've never learned any kind of dancing, much less square-dancing."

"Then, Alyce—I may call you that? Then it's time you learned. I'm not very expert myself, but you'll be changing partners enough not to mind too much."

Suddenly, Juan took my hand in his sculptured fingers, his dry palm clasped mine firmly. It was as if an unexpected loud sound had caused me to jump in surprise; I'd not anticipated his touch and it sent small waves of electricity-like sensations coursing through my body. He led me toward the circle of stomping, curtsying, dipping, whirling dancers, and broke us both into the chain before I realized it.

"Now hang on to your partner, she's a fine little girl,
"Show her you love her and give her a whirl!"

Juan's arm snaked around me, his palm resting with a light pressure in the center of my back. It was probably foolish of me, but I felt suddenly secure; almost, I imagined, what it must be like for a little girl to climb up on her father's lap. A private kingdom, a sense of well-being and of belonging.

Then, holding our hands high in the air, we two-stepped in a four-to-the-measure turn. Juan's torso was grazing against mine, but he was not offensively holding me too tightly. I stole a glance at his lean face, at the perfect straight nose and the eyes that seemed chiseled from dark marble. He led me as if we'd been dancing together all our lives, knew each other's every glide and pause. It was almost eerie how well we moved together, especially since I had never been graceful at dancing; yet in his arms I felt confident of every move—and I'd certainly never before been led in a square-dance. Under ordinary circumstances, I would have felt terribly out of place, embarrassed, and clumsy.

Glancing up at Juan's face, I saw that he was looking over the top of my head, as if scrutinizing the audience before the curtain went up. He seemed oblivious of my presence.

". . . Now turn to your neighbor, and give her a bow. . . ."

Suddenly, I was in another man's arms. He was a ruddy-faced youth, perhaps about eighteen or so, with a shock of reddish-brown hair, and a smile that would melt an iceberg. Small beads of perspiration were on his forehead, and his hands were a little sweaty, but he was such an engaging young man that I scarcely noticed it. "Pleased to meet you, ma'am," he said, just before passing me along to the next person—a woman, who curtsied, and I gathered I was to do the same . . . and then on to the next man. Clasping hands and walking smartly to the time of the music, we kept changing, swirling with a male partner, curtsying to a female, until the exchange had been completed. Some of the men seemed very shy, mumbling their "Nice to meet you" before moving on; others were boisterously enthusiastic, clamping my body against theirs as if I were about to fall over a precipice. The women were, for the most part, rather plain in appearance; but all of them had such a wholesomeness, an honest candor, about them that they became beautiful by their absence of guile or make-up.

I'd noted Juan along the chain, and he seemed to have something to converse about with everyone he encountered, smiling broadly, or—I was surprised to see—even laughing aloud. Perhaps Mary had been correct; perhaps Juan was overly formal until he got to know one better . . . yet, I couldn't help the nagging feeling that there was something about me he didn't like. I sensed a stiffness about him, a disapproval of me, which I couldn't quite understand. It was strange, really. His behavior would have seemed utterly normal and proper in Boston; but it struck me as cold and rude in this western atmosphere.

I wondered if his attitude was due to his being a Latin; the Spanish are known for their formality, I reasoned. Then I remembered Mary's remark about cubbyholing people, and swept the stereotyped thought beneath the carpet of my mind. No doubt Juan was merely uncomfortable with strangers, for which no ethnic group could claim priority—I was no different myself.

Just as I was beginning to become comfortable with recognizing the calls and their meaning, someone grabbed my arm and pulled me away from the circle of dancers, nearly causing me to lose my balance.

"You must be Alyce Laird!"

The blond man holding on to my arm swayed slightly, his pale blue eyes obviously attempting to focus on my face. His breath reeked of gin.

"You've gotta be! Only face I don't recognize!"

Everyone froze and watched this man as he grinned down

at me, his head bobbing occasionally in an obvious attempt to remain upright. I realized, of course, that he had to be Kyle Prescott.

"Hi, ever'one," he said, one arm gesturing in a wide sweep while his other hand still clenched my arm. "I'm a li'l late, I think."

Even as the words came out, Juan stepped forward and crossed over to us. "Let go of Alyce's arm," he said in a low, nearly menacing tone.

"What's it to you, Juanie-boy? You stake a claim on her for y'self or somethin'?"

Kyle Prescott weaved unsteadily, his eyes narrowing as he glowered at Juan—but he didn't let go of my arm, which was beginning to hurt from his vise-like grip.

"You're drunk, Kyle!" Juan hissed. "If you don't get your hands off of her right now . . ."

"Yeah? You'll wha'?"

Juan's fists clenched, the tendons in his neck ribbing tightly against his shirt collar. "Let go, Kyle, you're hurting her."

Kyle sneered in derision. "If I were hurtin' her, she'da said so, right? 'Sides, ya can't hit a man when he's drunk—'s'not fair!"

I tried to pull my arm away as discreetly as possible, but found that I couldn't. What worried me more, however, was the distinct possibility that the two of them were going to get into a fistfight with me right in the middle of the punches!

But at precisely that moment, Mary's husband, Dan, came stumbling to the barn door. His face was twisted in agony, silent sobs racking his body.

Alexander and William both rushed up to him at once. "What's the matter, Dan?" William demanded, concern etched across his face.

Dan Gomez stood leaning against the door frame, shaking his head from side to side as tears rolled down his cheeks. "Mary," he rasped hoarsely. "It's Mary!"

Then he slowly slid to the ground, covering his face with his hands as he broke into open, heartbreaking crying. William leaned over him, shaking him. "What about Mary? What's happened?"

The young man was inarticulate with obvious shock and

horror, yet he managed to point toward the house. "In . . . the . . . k-kitchen! My Maria, my darling Mary . . ."

Juan, William, and Alexander were the first to make a move, breaking into a run across the courtyard toward the dining-room doors. I don't know quite how, but I managed to get away from Kyle's grip, and followed them as quickly as my long skirt would permit. When I reached the kitchen, I couldn't absorb what my eyes beheld; my mind couldn't grapple with the scene.

There, sprawled halfway between the porch and the kitchen itself, lay Mary. Her eyes stared in glazed, unblinking death at the ceiling, her face frozen in terror, her lips parted to reveal a slowly swelling, black tongue. Her left arm, lying across the floor, was about three times its normal size, mottled and looking as if the flesh could not bear the inflammation much longer before it would burst.

Just beyond her, in the back porch, the snake slithered its way from the top of the garbage pail, wound its way toward Mary's ankles, then coiled and prepared to strike.

The four of us stood like statues, our eyes riveted to the horrible, terrifying mural of death before us. I was incapable of screaming. Although my mind was functioning, struggling to assimilate the panorama of terror before me, I felt mechanical, wooden. It was as if fear had converted me from a human being with feelings and emotions into some sort of electronic robot. My eyes were physically able to see; yet my electronic components couldn't compute what was before me.

No one moved.

The only sound in the room was the gourd-like sound of the snake's rattling tail, and the hissing noises as its forked tongue darted out its warning to us, its upper body and head undulating while its small black eyes never left us. It had curled itself beside Mary's leg, the way a pet cat might.

It watched us, waiting.

The hissing and rattling seemed interminable. At last, feeling myself garroted, my scream of horror tore through the room, through the night.

CHAPTER ELEVEN

Slivers of gray broke across the sky, slowly giving way to backlight the darker, heavy cumulus clouds that foretold of more snow to come during the day. I sat in Melanie's favorite armchair, numb physically, and inwardly turbulent. William had placed a cup of steaming black coffee in my hands, and I wrapped my fingers about it as if it made more sense than the world did.

I had no idea of the time, other than it was dawn. Dan had gone off with the deputy sheriff when Mary's body had been removed. Fortunately, Ben had been able to capture the Diamondback rattler using a snake stick and noose, then placing it in a collecting bag. Everyone had gone home, silent in their shock over Mary's death—and the cause of it. Only Juan and Kyle had remained on, though I wished that Kyle had left as well. While he seemed totally sober when I came to, I couldn't help associating his drunken intrusion with Mary's horrible death. Alexander and Ben had not permitted Melanie to come downstairs, telling her only that there had been an accident, that the party was breaking up early, and that she might as well just get a good night's rest. Daylight was approaching so rapidly, I knew she'd be downstairs soon—unaware, unprepared, and doubtlessly heartbroken by the news. She was such a gentle, peaceable soul; I knew she would have a difficult time coping with the news of Mary's untimely, totally unnecessary, death.

Alexander and William seemed disconsolate, not so much by the loss of Mary, but by the fact that the incident had occurred in their home. Kyle stood stony-faced by the dwindling fire, while Juan sat on the arm of the sofa, looking as though he might spring in any direction at a moment's notice. Little had been said until that moment; there seemed little one could say.

"Shall I put on another log?" Kyle said softly to no one in particular.

William shrugged, and Juan silently leaned over and took a log from the bin next to the fireplace and placed it atop the coals almost noiselessly. Then he turned and faced us all with an unfathomable expression. "Do you think it was one of Ben's snakes?" he inquired in a steady but nonaccusatory voice.

"Oh, for crissakes," Kyle muttered.

"No, he's right," William interjected. "We may as well discuss what's happened openly."

"He swears it wasn't," Alexander put in. "Or, at least, that he had nothing to do with it."

"Like the tarantula?" I said before I could stop myself.

"What tarantula!" Kyle demanded.

Alex swept nonexistent lint from his shirt sleeve. "We had a little incident about a week and a half ago. Nothing serious. Just typical of living in the area."

"It was in Melanie's bedroom," I said softly, ceasing to care about my status as a houseguest. Too much had happened and too soon, for me to even consider the amenities. "It bit her on the leg."

"That seems a rather strange coincidence," Kyle said, his full lips pulled into a tight line as he obviously connected the two events in his mind. "Tell us exactly what happened in the kitchen, Alyce, before you returned to the dance."

Mechanically, as if memorized by rote, I recited the events before rejoining the party. ". . . Then Juan came up behind me and asked me to dance, and that's all I can tell you."

"Behind you?" Kyle said.

Alex's eyes left my face to peer at Juan. "Why weren't you inside the barn with the others?"

Juan's gaze was steady, his resonant voice betraying the self-control he was exerting. "I'd been in the house in the lavatory," he said calmly. "Which, as you know," he added, directing himself to Kyle, "is in the opposite direction from the kitchen."

"Has anyone checked Ben's cellarful of pets to see if a Diamondback rattler is missing?" Kyle asked, ignoring Juan's barb.

"Even if it had been," William replied, "it wouldn't be by now. Assuming the worst, that it had been one of Ben's, he'd be back in his cage now. How would we know?"

"And the tarantula?" Juan asked.

"Who can tell, Juan," Alexander answered wearily. "He has dozens of them down there. Ben's a strange boy, but he's not a liar. He said he knew nothing about either incident, and I believe him."

"You're his father," Kyle reminded. "And Ben's not a boy anymore, he's my age. At thirty-three, you're not just a boyish prankster."

I only half listened to the conversation, sensing, more than actually knowing, that it was going nowhere. Gazing out the living-room window, a dull tangerine glow began to show itself along the tips of the snow-covered mountains and I was dully glad to realize it would not be a totally overcast day. I couldn't have stood a gray day—not after what had happened.

"It seems to me," William said, tilting his head backward as if he were carrying an enormous weight, "that we're all skirting a distinct possibility."

"Such as?" Kyle asked.

"Such as the two events being deliberate attempts to frighten or kill someone . . . and making them look like Ben's fault."

There was a long silence, and William's words burned in my mind. Somehow, in some subconscious manner, I'd suspected this possibility and had been unable to let it surface. "But why Melanie?" I blurted. "Who'd want to harm her?"

Alex let himself fall into his chair, rubbing his eyes slowly with his strong, thick fingers. "Of course! I should have realized it."

"Realized what?" I asked.

"The night of the tarantula, both of your bedroom doors were somewhat ajar," William answered. "That spider could have been placed in *your* room earlier in the evening . . . and it simply crossed over into Melanie's. It was never meant to be in Melanie's room. . . ."

"And last night," Alexander added, "might have been a repeat of the same thing. No one could have foretold that Mary would be in the kitchen helping you and Melanie—but it was a safe bet that *you* would."

"Are you saying someone's trying to kill Alyce?" Juan asked.

"But who . . . and why?" I asked, my body tensing at the conjecture.

"To frighten you away," William replied softly.

"No one knew I was here, other than us," I protested.

William smiled. "The whole Los Padres National Forest knew you were here before you and Ben even got back from checking you out of the hotel! This isn't a big city, Alyce. You'd stopped to talk to the realtor, Hank, who knew you were looking for Manny. Not many city people come up here to look him up, and especially not all the way from the East. Manny knew it, of course, and moreover, knew just why you were here."

"There's only one road in and out of Frazier, Alyce. With Ben following you in his car, and the two of you returning together in the same day . . . in an area as lightly populated as this is, that's news!" Alexander contributed.

Juan nodded solemnly. "They're right, of course. The locals were telling me about the Musser houseguest within twenty-four hours of your arrival. They may not have known who you were, or why you were visiting, Alyce, but they knew you were from the East and were busily piecing together the connection between Mansfield Watersdown, you, and the Musser family."

"But . . . but other than local gossip, what could it possibly matter to anyone?" I persisted, my eyes riveted to Juan's handsome face, until Alexander cleared his throat pointedly and shot me a warning glance to be silent.

"Well, I think the whole theory is idiotic," Kyle said deprecatingly. "Two accidents in such a short period is doubtlessly coincidental. In both cases, they involved creatures that are part of the natural habitat. There's not a resident in this area who doesn't know to be careful about spiders and insects in the cupboards and dark corners of a house. We're all accustomed to it! I think you're letting fancy overcome good sense."

"Perhaps because of the shock of Mary's death," William said contemplatively. "If anything, Melanie would seem to be the one who's in danger, not Alyce—and we all know no one could wish Melanie any harm."

I had a sudden, fervent need to see Manny, to talk to someone who was calmly logical. I was beginning to feel claustrophobic in that room, a panic welling up within me that threatened to become hysteria if I didn't speak with someone who had my interests at heart. Oh Mother, I thought, forcing myself not to let the tears surface, what can I do? Shall I stay here, in this strange, alien forest where deadly creatures lurk —and kill . . . ? This area you loved so much is evil and hostile toward me. There's so much I don't understand, so much that has happened here in the years you were away. Would you want me to stay on, if you were alive and here? Are the threats that drove you away now being directed toward me? The walls seemed to be crushing in on me, and the voices of the men speculating on deliberate action versus accident seemed to come to me from another room, my ears filtering the sounds in a gossamer of fear.

✳☙✳

"Yes, I'd just heard about it moments before you drove up," Manny said, pouring us both freshly brewed coffee. "Mrs. Cayard phoned me 'bout it not even half an hour ago. Poor Dan, he adored Maria. He won't get over her death any too quickly. Funeral's been set for Monday."

He placed a warm, gnarled hand on my shoulder. "Have you had any breakfast? You're looking mighty wan, and you'd best keep your strength up if you're to be of any use to anyone—yourself included."

I shook my head at his offer. The thought of eating anything was beyond me. Borrowing Ben's car, I'd driven back to the town of Frazier and barged in on Mansfield Watersdown like a child rushing to Grandpa for comforting. "Manny," I began slowly, "I'm afraid. I don't know if it's for Melanie or for my own safety—but I'm afraid."

He lowered himself slowly into the chair facing me, tamping his tobacco and lighting his pipe with shaking hands and an air of premeditated stalling. "Want to go back to Boston?"

"I don't know," I said honestly. "I have to talk to you, to someone who can tell me if I'm being melodramatic or childish—or smart enough to want to save my own neck."

He nodded, puffing gently on his pipe. "Seems logical. After what's happened, you'd have to be pretty stupid not to question what to do next."

I leaned forward, searching his face for some sign of guidance. "What do you think I should do?"

His smile was almost wistful. "Hard to advise you, Alyce. If you want to claim your share of the gold mine, you'll have to stay here. If you are seriously worried that someone's trying to kill you, to scare you off . . . then I think there's no amount of money in the world you can spend in the grave!"

"But do *you* think these are threats? Or just coincidence?"

Manny sighed heavily. "I'm just a lawyer, Alyce. We tend to think in rather pedantic ways, go by the book, so to speak. So far, nothing's happened that couldn't have been purely accidental. On the other hand, *if* either Kyle or Juan has guessed why you're here . . . they could be threats. A fatal threat for Mary Gomez, as it turns out."

"Oh, Manny, you're equivocating!"

"Well, dammit girl! What do you want? Do you think I should point a finger at someone and accuse him of trying to kill you or Melanie?" Manny's eyes snapped with impatience.

"You're right," I said after a moment. "I'm sorry. I'm just so terribly upset since Mary's death . . . I guess I'm not being very practical." I hoped my expression conveyed my apology better than my tone of voice. "It isn't just the money. . . ."

"Alyce, Alyce," Manny drawled. "Why don't you just go back East to your regular life. There's nothing here for you but possible danger. Life is different out here. It's harsh and hard. It takes a very special kind of person to be able to live in this forest . . . you're a city girl. Your mother was a woman of enormous endurance and perseverance. When she set her mind to something, that was it—nothing stopped her. But you're not your mother, nor should you have to pretend to be. There's nothing wrong with being a city person. . . ."

"Are you saying I'm a coward?" I demanded hotly. I could feel my whole being bristling at Manny's implication.

"No, I'm not! Now simmer down! I've had some time to think over your reason for coming here, and I've had some second thoughts! Now if you'll just calm down for a moment, I'll explain them to you; but if you're going to go off all half-baked in adolescent indignation, then don't bother me with your problems!"

Had Mansfield Watersdown slapped me soundly across the face, I couldn't have sobered more quickly. I felt like a fool, my body drained of strength.

"That's better," Manny said gently. "Now then, let me give you some conclusions I've come to. For one thing, I think you were right when you reminded us that neither Kyle nor Juan would have any actual recollection of what their fathers may or may not have done. So if you don't find some kind of physical evidence in the form of a diary or letters, some kind of dummying up of the ledgers, you don't stand a chance of proving anything. Even if Kyle and Juan *know* what happened to your father, they're not about to admit it."

"Go on," I said, considerably mollified.

"Secondly, even if you were to find some kind of evidence or even proof, that means going to court with it. You'd have to be here for at least a year before you'd get a preliminary hearing, the way court dates are backed up in Fresno. And even at that, you couldn't afford to hire the kind of attorneys either of the boys could. I couldn't help you, Alyce. Even if I weren't retired, I'm just too damned old to get in there and outsmart, and outfight, a younger lawyer. Thirdly, if you *lost* the case, you'd be putting yourself straight in line for a libel suit!"

I slumped in the chair, disheartened, beaten. "Then you think my best move is to go back where I came from."

"I do."

I lighted a cigarette, my hands none too steady, as I mulled over Manny's advice. It seemed like valid guidance, as if he'd taken all possibilities under consideration and had come up with a sane, sensible conclusion. Yet, there was something pat about it; something that nagged at the perimeter of my awareness. While it all had the surface gloss of common sense, yet something within me was resisting the idea of just packing up and leaving Frazier; just forgetting about the whole thing.

Thanking Manny for his trouble and concern, I got back into Ben's car just as a fresh, heavy snow was beginning. The promise of sunlight at dawn was now coated over with pendulous billows of gray cloud. I waved good-bye to Manny and edged my way slowly out of his rutted driveway back down to the main road, Mount Pinos Way. By then the snow was falling so rapidly, the windshield wipers were having trouble scraping it off. I put the defroster on to its fullest, but it wasn't doing very much to clear the windshield; and vision out the rear window was impossible—it sat there like a blind eye rolled back in its socket.

I'd driven too far by then to try to get back to Manny's, and in truth, I wasn't too sure I wanted to. I needed time to think about what he'd said . . . time to sort through and make up my own mind.

Peering through the windshield as best I could, listening to the sandpaper-like rasping of the rubber blades trying to cut through the icy snow adhering to the windshield, I leaned over the steering wheel straining to see the road. The pitch of the road itself had long since disappeared, but I was using the gullies on either side of the road to guide me as I edged my way at less than ten miles per hour. Though not even noon yet, the sky was so ominously dark it seemed apocalyptic in its warning.

Wending my way slowly, straining with every nerve in my body, I tried desperately to follow what I hoped was the road. The world had become a white crypt, and I was a mere ant attempting to surmount the insurmountable. I creeped for another mile, perhaps a little more, realizing in my heart that it was a hopeless situation—I'd simply have to abandon the attempt and hope that someone would be out with plows soon. Yet, doggedly, I kept on going, hoping against hope I'd somehow get through.

Then I felt the right front wheel slowly sinking into the snow, the car settling into the innocent-looking whiteness like a behemoth into a virgin marsh, and I knew that was it. I must have driven off the road—who knew how long ago?—and had now hit a gully of some sort. I was sick with my own pigheaded stupidity. Glancing at the gas gauge, I saw there was a little under a quarter of a tank. Ample enough gasoline for a direct line between El Fin del Camino and Manny's cabin—but not for trying to drive across Los Padres National Forest without a sled! While there was enough to leave the engine running for a little while, and keeping myself warm, I could envision myself being slowly snowed in beyond hope of rescue.

With the way it was coming down, the whole car could be totally camouflaged from view within another hour—and I would be trapped in it. I had no choice but to get out and walk . . . and pray that I was walking in the right direction!

CHAPTER TWELVE

I had seen many snowstorms in my life, but I'd never witnessed anything like the blizzard that raged about me as I fought to traverse the eiderdown that would not support my one hundred and ten pounds. Often, my foot would sink into the snow and I'd find my leg knee-deep in the wet, clinging coldness. It didn't take long to learn not to put my full weight on each new step until I saw how far I would sink, and it was only with a wrenching effort that I was able to drag out the other leg from the last step. It also didn't take much intelligence to realize it could take me days to reach shelter at my rate of sluggish progress. Since it had been snowing off and on for more than a week, this latest cascade that whipped and danced about me left drifts halfway up tree trunks that were at least thirty feet high.

That I was hopelessly lost was obvious. The forest had thickened, and there wasn't a house to be seen anywhere through the white gauze of the storm. I was so wet, so cold, I was almost beyond caring. My eyes felt frozen in their sockets, and I'd long since lost any sensation in my feet; the pain in my ears felt like stilettos had been driven through the drums, and while I was wearing gloves, they'd never been meant as protection against this kind of exposure. At one point, I'd thought to retrace my steps and return to the car—it had to be safer than this aimless wandering and threat of freezing to death. Yet, when I looked back, only the most recent footprints could be discerned with certainty; the other indentations could have been just the terrain itself. Obviously, going back or even attempting to would be more stupid than my initial decision to leave the car. I cursed myself as all manner of a fool, asking myself why I'd not just opened the car door to ensure my escape should it prove necessary, letting the engine's warmth—for as long as the gasoline lasted—ward off being buried alive or freezing to death. Even with an open door, the car heater would still be better than what I was presently enduring.

Naturally, I'd no idea of how long I'd been trenching along —an hour? Two? I didn't know. It felt like days!

Then, as I rounded a huge pine laden with snow, I thought I saw something black in the distance, something squarish in appearance. A house? A forester's lookout? I couldn't be sure, but I decided to head for it. Distance was terribly deceptive in a blizzard, and I prayed with all my heart that, whatever that black hope was, it wasn't too far away. I seriously doubted that I could endure much more, and I needed no reference book to tell me what would happen if I stopped to rest a few moments; the overwhelming sleepiness, the frozen circulation, the loss of will to live . . . while it would be a relatively painless death, it would nonetheless be my permanent nap of death.

Doggedly, I tramped toward that black square, that last hope of my survival, and took some measure of comfort in noting that it was drawing closer, getting larger. At least the wind had shifted, and I was no longer pitching headlong into it. Now, it came in great gusts from my right, occasionally knocking me over, but I kept my eyes squinted at that yawning square and kept going. Thoughts of Christmas cards, of quaint New England winter scenes, flashed through my mind sardonically; how could anything so beautiful as snow be so lethal, so relentlessly cruel! I thought of my mother, and of Manny's description of her as a determined, unswervable person, practically a pioneer in this wilderness—and it aided my resolve to take another step, yet another, just a few more . . . keep going, Alyce, keep going . . . you're not far now . . . one step at a time, just another, you're doing fine, Alyce Prather Laird, your mother would be proud of you. . . .

At long last, I was able to make out what the blackness was: a shaft. Some kind of a mine, I thought, and nearly cried

with relief. It would be cold, but not as cold as in the thick of
the blizzard, buffeted like a stick in the driving winds. I could
sit down on dry earth . . . rest! Oh God! How the anticipation
spurred me onward! I tore at the drifts, clinging to any shrub
for support, pushing myself from tree trunks for impetus—I'd
have swum through the snow, had it been possible. Hope lay
ahead. My survival was just beyond. Once I slipped and
rolled several feet down a slope before I clutched at a boulder
to stop my fall. Breathing heavily, the fog of my body warmth
pumping from my gasping breath as I tried to bring my heart-
beat under control, I climbed back up again, hand over hand,
mindless of the shreds that were once gloves on my hands.

Impeded by the long woolen skirt I still wore from the
night before, I laboriously pulled up its sopping weight and
tucked the hem of it inside the waistband. My legs were red
and raw-looking, swollen to nearly twice their normal size. I'd
long since lost the shoes I'd been wearing for the dance. The
dance, I thought. When was that? How many weeks ago?
Would I ever dance again? Would the frostbite necessitate—
no! I wouldn't think about that! It was too horrible to contemplate. I began to write my own obituary in my head to keep
myself going, to remind myself of how vital it was to keep
moving, to reach that mine . . . one step . . . another step
. . . keep going, keep going. . . .

Finally, virtually crawling up the incline, I reached the
mouth of the mine and hurled myself with my last bit of
strength across the rocky dirt floor of it, mindless of the abra-
sions on legs I could no longer feel, and I began to sob with
gratitude and relief. How long I lay like that, I don't know.
The tears rolled down my frozen flesh, thawing snow as they
flowed, my body racked with the tidal wave of release. When
my crying finally subsided, every muscle in my body ached
with the unaccustomed wrenching of my torso. Unashamedly
whimpering by then, I forced myself into a sitting position.
My legs looked like hamburger; scratched badly, but the
blood had frozen before it had a chance to flow. I slowly
reached down and touched my thigh. There was no sensation
whatsoever. I touched my calf; it reacted with a dull tingling,
almost a burning sensation. I knew I'd not be able to stand on
them for quite some time—I only hoped it wouldn't be forever

due to their amputation . . . *if* anyone ever found me in this abandoned cave.

I glanced about in the gloomy darkness, this shelter which could prove to be my tomb. Aside from the howling of the wind, all I was aware of was that I was no longer out there, and while my breathing was labored and shallow, at least I was still breathing. Grasping at the wall of the mine, I dragged myself for a few feet farther into the cave. With an elation bordering on a mystical experience, I found some neatly piled two-by-fours and enough broken planks and splinters to make a fire. The wood was very old, probably as old as the mine itself, which meant it would be dry and would ignite easily.

Fumbling frantically, in a state of near hysteria, I laughed aloud as I reached inside my parka pocket and sought my cigarettes and lighter. Yes . . . *yes!* I could just manage with fingers barely able to obey . . . slowly, don't rush! Don't lose your slight grip on the lighter . . . easy, easy . . . ! My mind raced with commands and enforced calmness while I struggled to disgorge the precious lighter from the pocket. At long last, I had it in my palm, and I laughed yet again. Mother may have disapproved of my smoking, but it was about to save my life! Feebly, gingerly, I spun the flint wheel. If it even sparked, my eyes failed to perceive it. I ordered my conscious self not to panic, to be logical; of course it wouldn't work right away—the parts were doubtlessly frozen, though I was confident the fluid had too much alcohol, or whatever butane is made from, to have frozen as well. My mind struggled with a solution for a few moments, until it occurred to me to place the small lighter beneath my parka next to my bosom— my own body warmth, such as it was, would thaw the lighter.

While waiting for the lighter to warm up, I did my best to make some sort of teepee out of the smaller pieces of wood. Once ignited, I could drag the larger two-by-four across it and let the fire itself burn the piece in half. There were plenty of the larger pieces, but very little of the kindling; I would have to be judicious lest I use it all up before I could get a healthy fire going. If I get out of this alive, I thought, I'll make a donation to the Girl Scouts out of every paycheck! If only Mother had permitted me to join when I was a girl, half of my fears could have been assuaged. I'd no idea of how to build a fire other than what I'd seen in movies, or watched others do in their own hearths—usually assisted with a modern gas starter.

When the teepee was complete, and after enormous effort I'd managed to drag two of the larger timbers within reach, I again took out my cigarette lighter. With trembling hands and fingers that felt as if they'd been caught in a blender, I flicked the lighter. It sparked, but did not ignite. I found myself staring at it like a naughty child. "Light, damn you, light!" I swore at it and tried again. Gleefully, I watched the small instrument respond to my command, the flickering flame the most welcome sight in my entire life.

Slowly leaning forward lest too rapid a movement would extinguish the flame, I placed it beneath the kindling and waited. I tried to remember how long I'd had this particular lighter; the disposable ones never lasted too terribly long and since its construction was of an opaque plastic, I couldn't tell by looking at the fluid level. I closed my eyes, momentarily praying that it had sufficient fluid to get the kindling going.

I began to feel warmth, then heat against my hand. When I again opened my eyes, small flames were licking upward on the kindling. I allowed the lighter to drop to the ground and, as quickly as I was able to move, placed another piece of kindling against the flame. In a short while, the fire was strong enough for me to risk dragging the two-by-four across the center of it. The feeble warmth of it in the bitterly cold mine was sufficient to sear my tortured flesh; the mere hint of heat reacted upon my frostbitten flesh like a blowtorch, but I didn't care. It was heat; it was a chance to survive, to live through this nightmare. I stared at the flames, willing them to eat through the larger strut. Whether from exhaustion, exposure, or even the hypnotic effect of the capricious flames, my eyes became weary beyond control; my eyelids felt as if great weights were pulling them closed—and I knew no more.

✳⠋✳

I awakened as if drugged, wondering if I'd lost my sanity—I was certain I could hear a man softly singing "This is the way we wash our clothes, wash our clothes. . . ." I sensed, rather than felt, that things were—well, different. Not as I'd remembered. Snowstorm. Leave car. Trek across the Himalayas. Abandoned mine. Make fire.

". . . So early in the morning!"

With my eyes still shut, I took inventory of my body. There was now some sensation in my limbs, though not much. I didn't feel wet or cold, though. How could that be? The fire? Had I slept so long my clothes had dried out? Clothes! I didn't have my clothes on! Just my underwear. Blanket! Yes, there was definitely a blanket covering me! Where was I? The smell of burning wood was strong in my nostrils. Then a man's voice humming the child's melody; sounds of heavy boots upon the rock-strewn dirt floor of the mine, moving about methodically.

I opened one eye.

Snowshoes were stacked against the far wall of the cave. Knee-high laced boots encased a man's trousered legs with feet well planted upon the ground. The hem of my woolen skirt dangling near the flame of the robust fire. A compact grill had been placed over the flames, with a freckled enamel pan on top of it. My eyes roamed upward as I tried to assimilate what in the world was happening, or had happened!

A nylon cord was strung across the width of the shaft; layered across it was my skirt, my blouse, and my parka. Kyle Prescott was doing his best to smooth out the wrinkles in the skirt, then turned his head in a way that suggested he'd been doing just that for quite some time, checking to see how I was.

"Awake, are you?" he asked cheerfully. I found myself unable to utter a sound. "Well, let me tell you, Alyce Laird, you look a sight—but at least you'll pull through."

"I . . . wha . . . ?"

"Feel up to a bit of broth?" he asked, kneeling down and taking a tin cup from a backpack near his snowshoes. "Figured if I found you at all, you'd not be in very good condition, so I brought along a few vittles, as we say in this part of the country."

He handed me the cup, which I accepted with aching limbs and incredulous eyes. I raised it to my lips and let the warmth of its steam travel through my nose, hoping to unclog my brain. When I tried to press the rim to my lips, I soon realized they were grotesquely swollen and blistered, and I winced at the contact.

"Oh, you're a mess, all right." Kyle laughed. "But I don't think we'll have to hospitalize you . . . or cut off either of those lovely legs of yours," he added. "Sorry, but I had to get those wet clothes off of you, and, well, I *am* a man. You *do* have great legs, and I couldn't help noticing."

With great care, I sipped on the hot bouillon, my brain beginning to function again. "Surprised you didn't bring a St. Bernard and a brandy keg," I managed to say finally.

"Wrong! One of the biggest misconceptions known to man! Anything alcoholic is the worst possible thing you can give to someone damned-near frozen through and through."

"It is?"

He nodded sagely. "While it raises the body temperature a bit, it's only because it sends more blood to the surface of the skin—which, of course, is closer to the freezing temperature. Worse, it deprives the vital organs of sufficient blood to continue working under the deadly circumstances. Are you impressed?"

His smile was so self-satisfied I couldn't resist being amused. Both of us were behaving as if there were nothing at all unusual about two people stranded in an abandoned mine in the middle of a blizzard. We might have been having high tea at the Savoy, the way we were talking. Finally, my curiosity took over. "How in earth did you find me?"

Kyle was still squatting near the fire, pulling another cup out of his backpack and an enormous can of beans, which he proceeded to open with a small device, then placed it atop the grill over the fire. He winked at me, pouring himself a cup of broth as well. "When you didn't come back, naturally we all became concerned. Alexander reasoned that you must have gone to see Mansfield Watersdown, since you don't know anyone else around here."

"Yes, but how did you find me in here?" I persisted.

Kyle stirred the beans in the can with an aluminum spoon. "Alyce . . . I've got as many faults as the next man, maybe more. But I'll thank you not to interrupt me when I'm in the middle of a yarn." He tested the temperature of the beans, stirred them yet again, then put the spoon on a rock nearby. "Now then, as I was saying. William began to wonder if maybe you hadn't returned to L.A.—especially after Mary's death last night. Then Juan telephoned Manny and learned that you'd left only a few moments before; half an hour at the most, according to Manny. So, we waited and waited *and* waited. We'd all been talking so much about the way Mary had died that none of us had really noticed the blizzard. We're sort of used to that type of thing around here."

I was ready to strangle Kyle Prescott by then, but in view of how he had doubtlessly saved my life, I kept my silence.

"Finally, Juan noticed the storm and between us we figured out what must've happened. We alerted the Forestry boys, and the three of us split up into separate, individual hunting parties."

"The three of you?"

"Yeah, William, Juan, and me. We found Ben's car about thirty yards off the road, but your tracks had long since been covered over, so we split up in different directions."

"Then they're still out there looking for me?" I shuddered at the thought!

Kyle shook his head. "They'd have gone home by now. It's almost seven o'clock now and entirely too dark to even try."

"But now they'll think you're missing too," I blurted with guilt-ridden supposition.

"Doubt it. We all grew up in these mountains, we know how to take care of ourselves. What they don't know is that I've found you, and that you're safe." He rose, felt the state of my clothes, then reversed them on the line so the other side could benefit from the warmth of the fire. "I figured that if I didn't find you dead, you might have made it to this old mine. When I spotted the smoke coming out of it, I knew I would find you here. You're a very lucky gal, Alyce! If the wind had shifted, you'd have suffocated in here."

"I'd have suffocated," I repeated with incredulous irony. "I was about to freeze to death out *there!* What were my choices?"

Kyle laughed. "Yeah, but don't you know anything at all about survival tactics? Any first-grader knows to check for an airshaft before making a fire in a cave or a mine like this! That was really pretty stupid of you!"

I was so outraged I couldn't form a protest, but merely blustered while searching for words. It didn't matter that I was exhausted, or that Kyle had come to my rescue; I couldn't believe his effrontery in the face of the facts!

"Okay, okay, calm down."

At last words came to me. "If I'm stupid, why do you still have the fire going?"

"See how I've hung your clothes? See how it forms some kind of wall to block off the rest of the mine?"

I nodded slowly.

"Well, forget it." He grinned. "The fire's still going 'cause I don't want to freeze to death either." He leaned over and pulled out a package from his backpack. "Ready for some dinner?"

I was so dumbstruck I didn't know what to say. What kind of man was this Kyle Prescott? A rude drunk on first meeting, a devil-may-care rescuer the next. A rogue, a woodsman? Whatever he was, he certainly wasn't a simple, noncomplex individual. While he unwrapped the package, pulling a hunting knife from his belt to slice what looked like sausage, I observed him more carefully. Contrary to the almost weathered face of Juan Melendez, Kyle had a boyish, wrinkle-free face; his jaw wasn't quite as prominent as Juan's, and I wondered if the full cheeks might not be due to overindulgence with drinking. His hair was not as carefully groomed now, but that was to be expected after tramping through a snowstorm. There was an aura about Kyle that made me think he should be a Madison Avenue executive on his way up: a young but slowly dissipating expression on his face—a little bored, a little cynical, and yet there was strength in his features. I had the impression that Kyle Prescott was on the brink, teetering between two possible worlds: complete abandonment to the life of a playboy, or wrestling with himself to make something of his life.

"Here," he said abruptly, "have some beef jerky. You won't like it much, but there's a lot of nourishment in it. We'll have to share the can of beans. I didn't have room for plates in my pack. Figured the amenities could be sacrificed for food and warmth."

He handed me the dried meat at the tip of his knife and I took it, mindful of the glistening blade. "Do you think they'll find us tomorrow?" I asked.

"Uh-huh," he mouthed chewing on the tough meat. "They'll see the smoke from the cave and the Forestry boys will send in a rescue crew with a litter for you."

"I . . . I want to, to thank you, Kyle," I began.

"Hey! Forget it!" he said lightly. "I'd have done the same thing for anyone."

"But you don't even know me, not really, and to risk your life . . ."

Kyle waved aside my attempted thanks. "I felt I sort of owed it to you," he said slowly.

"Owed it?" I asked, my perplexity evident in my voice.

He moved over closer to me, bringing the can of beans with him and placing it directly between us as he rested his back against the rough wall, then handed me a spoon of my own. "Look," he began softly. "Both Juan and I grew up with the whispers about our fathers doing in your dad. Whenever we'd get into a fight at school, some kid would call one or both of us sons of murderers. This whole area has gossiped about your father's death ever since I can remember, falling suddenly silent if Juan or I should enter the room. They never speak to us directly about it, mind you, that would be too honest. Just the hushed tones about how our parents murdered your father in order to get the gold mine away from him."

His voice had become tight, resentful, and trailed off into silence. I could well appreciate how awful it would be to grow up under those circumstances.

"So, anyway," he resumed, back to his jocular self again, "at least the natives can't say we tried to kill you off too."

"Why would you want to?" I asked, but was already afraid of his answer.

"To stop you from proving the gossipers right."

"Is that what you think I'm here to do?"

"Aren't you?"

"Is there any way I could?" I asked softly.

Kyle paused with a spoonful of beans halfway to his mouth, looking into my eyes steadily. "Yes."

"Will you tell me how?"

Kyle smiled strangely. "I can tell you how, but I won't help you. And I doubt strongly that Juan would either."

I said nothing, hoping my silence would draw him out. Despite the tenseness of the moment, beyond the knowledge that I could possibly accomplish what I'd come West to do, my fatigue was returning in nausea-producing shocks throughout my body. Again, I felt the terrible heaviness in my limbs, my eyes barely able to remain open. While the broth had felt good, the beef was making me slightly sick and the beans tasted like mush. I forced myself to concentrate, to stick with the subject. "Why not?"

Kyle's head tilted at me as he obviously took in my weakening condition. He made a little clucking noise, as if weighing his alternatives, then sighed heavily. "One of our fathers kept a journal. We don't know which one. And we don't know where it is. Most of the time, Juan and I don't get along very well, but about that journal . . . we've been in accord since we were boys. We don't want to find it. We don't want to know the truth. While neither of us knows for sure, neither of us has to be ashamed. It's that simple."

I heard him say "simple" and then drifted off back to sleep. At some point during the restless, howling night, I thought I'd felt a man's beard against my face, lips gently kissing my swollen, blistered own . . . but I thought I must be dreaming it. Who'd want to kiss a frostbitten, thirty-year-old spinster from Boston?

CHAPTER THIRTEEN

My recollection of the next day is quite hazy. As predicted, the Forestry rescue team showed up, and I was carried out of the shaft in a canvas litter. It was still snowing, but it was a gentle, playful snowfall; as if it had a will of its own and was coquettishly making amends for its severity the previous day. I knew I had a raging fever, and I was only dimly aware of what was happening around me. Kyle barked a few instructions to the others, but it meant nothing to me; I didn't know why Kyle sounded so angry, and I didn't even care. I was too sick to care about anything, actually.

Then, somehow, I found myself awakening inside a hospital room—which I knew was impossible since there was no hospital in Frazier, so I attributed my environs to feverish delusions —slept again, awakened later and thought I saw Kyle in the corner of the room, slept again. This type of in-and-out consciousness went on endlessly, it seemed. I imagined I heard a doctor's voice, then on some other occasion, I thought I heard Kyle and Juan Melendez arguing in a heated whisper. At one point, I was visiting my mother's gravesite, watching workmen erect an enormous tombstone of white marble; it was a mammoth bird of some kind—but then it seemed to enter a metamorphosis and became a griffin, and it flew away leaving an empty pedestal at the head of my mother's grave.

Finally, I awoke and found myself feeling quite lucid, quite aware of my situation. I was, to be sure, in a hospital. Seated across from my bed was Melanie, crocheting something with total concentration. She could have been transplanted to the

Lincoln Memorial and not known the difference. I smiled slowly, watching her dear face as her expression would change depending upon what she was thinking, or doing. ". . . Melanie," I began to say and realized I was barely able to talk. I tried to move my left arm and became aware of the i.v. connected to it, but the movement was sufficient to divert Melanie's attention to me.

"Land sakes, child, why didn't you say you were awake!"

She leaped from the chair and bent over me, concern and relief written across her kindly, round face.

"I—I tried," I managed to croak out. "W-where am I?"

Melanie lifted my head gingerly, puffing the pillows beneath me, and gently helping me to sit up a little. "You're in Bakersfield General Hospital," she said, "and you've had all of us worried sick! I'm so angry with Mansfield Watersdown I don't think I can ever bring myself to speak to him again!"

"W-what did he do?" I rasped.

"What did he *do!* Why, gracious, he should've known better than to let you go out in that storm! He knows this country and knows what kind of storms we get around here, and to have let you go out like that was . . . was—well, in *my* opinion, it was akin to attempted murder!"

Despite my feeble condition, I found myself smiling. Melanie did have a way of taking the slightest incident and turning it into a soap opera. It was pointless to try to dissuade Melanie from her outraged opinion; not only was I too weak and unable to speak, but Melanie—like our mother—had that tight-lipped set to her jaw that indicated argument would be useless. She would get over it in time, I was certain, and I could reason with her on some other occasion. I elected to change the subject. "How . . . long h-have I been here?"

Melanie straightened up, clasping her hands together tightly beneath her bosom. "Six days now. You've been in a coma, with a temperature that reached a hundred and six, and even Doc Adams was worried you might not pull through the pneumonia. Had you in an oxygen tent most the time, but we've all taken turns sitting with you. This hospital's about the best in this entire area, but it's terribly understaffed. Finding a nurse around here's like trying to find a yellow thread in a haystack."

She'd been mid-sentence when a freshly starched R.N. entered the room, eyebrows raised archly at Melanie's words. "Feeling a little better?" she asked me, ignoring Melanie altogether. "Good. Your family's been quite concerned," she said, stressing the word "family" as if Melanie were a stranger to me. "I'll let Dr. Adams know you're conscious now. Lucky for you he's on call today."

"And I'll use the payphone down the hall to let Alex and William know you've come to and are feeling a bit better." Melanie whisked past the nurse with her upturned nose in the air. I'd never been a patient in a hospital before, and I found it surprising that such bickering between a nurse and a family member would transpire in the sickroom. I tried to sit up a bit, pressing my palms against the firm mattress, only to find that I didn't have the strength to move my own body.

"Here, I'll prop the bed up," the nurse said efficiently, then bent over and cranked the upper third of the bed to a more comfortable sitting position. Before I could even thank her, she had whipped out a thermometer, given it a couple of neck-breaking jerks, and inserted it into my mouth. "I'm Nurse Redfield," she said abruptly, "and if you need me for anything, here's the buzzer button. It's connected to the main station on this floor, which is attended twenty-four hours a day. Miss Musser is correct about our being understaffed," she said stiffly, "however we are doing the best we can. We are also asking our patients to avoid needless requests, such as getting a magazine for them. Try to anticipate your needs as best you can so we can consolidate various requests in one trip."

I tried to talk through the thermometer and when I saw the horrified expression on Nurse Redfield's face, I acquiesced and nodded instead.

"If Dr. Adams will permit you to go on solid foods this evening, I'll be back to find out what you'd prefer from our limited menu. Now then, about breakfast," she said in a tone that made breakfast sound like medication, while glancing at her watch, then removing the thermometer from my mouth. She squinted at it, then jotted down my temperature on the chart at the foot of the bed. "Coffee or tea?" she demanded from me.

"Coffee," I replied, not really able to contemplate such a distant event. No wonder most people spoke the way they did about a hospital stay! Nurse Redfield made me feel as if I were a convict, and she was merely giving me a list of my rights.

She busied herself a little more and left within seconds of Melanie's return. "Alex is so pleased to hear how you've improved," she said, pleasure and pride glimmering in her child-like blue eyes. "He said they'll be over after supper and keep you company."

"I'm s-sorry to have put you all through all this worry," I managed to say. Every word was an effort to get out, and I was rapidly reaching a plateau of weightlessness.

"Wasn't your fault, child. It was that man's, whose name I don't wish to mention at this moment in time. But doesn't matter now. What matters is that you're better, and I'm sure Doc Adams will let you come home as soon as you're able. He should be here any second now; I spotted him just down the hall doing his rounds."

"And is Kyle all right?" I asked hesitantly.

"Kyle? Land sakes, Alyce, he's just fine, just fine. Been here every day, the boys tell me, just sitting in this chair and watching over you. Why, I don't think Kyle's had a drink since he found you in that awful mine. Wasn't that a stroke of luck though? Kyle's like that, though. Goes off God-knows-where for days, sometimes weeks—drunk, most likely—and then he can turn around and be just the nicest, most considerate person in town. He's a strange one. Needs to marry up with a sensible young woman and settle down," Melanie concluded neatly, with a significant glance in my direction. Obviously, she had elected me for the post of sensible wife for Kyle Prescott.

I felt myself drifting off, an overwhelming sense of disinterest pervading my entire being. I tried desperately to focus on Melanie's face, her closely cropped gray-brown hair, but it was no use. My eyelids kept coming together like a magnet and a hairpin, inexorably sealed by joint consent. Sounds faded and became distant, and I floated into another dimension of timelessness, fantasy, and dreams. Kyle? Kyle who! And onto the mural of my subconscious thoughts, I again saw

Juan as he was that night of the square dance; saw him with fists clenched, warning Kyle to let me go or . . . Or? Would Juan have struck Kyle to protect me? Or would he have backed off, not deigning to stoop to adolescent physical violence? And why should Kyle be such a muddle of contradictions? Kyle. Handing me that awful beef jerky on the tip of his hunting knife, the blade glistening with lethal menace in the reflected fire glow.

One of our fathers kept a journal.

We don't know which one.

Come back, griffin! Don't leave my mother all alone!

Then you march straight upstairs, Mary had said to Melanie. *And you, Alyce, you go on back to the party.* But Mary was dead. A horrible, agonizing death. The eyes! The rattler's beady glistening eyes! Had it known? Had it seen at once it had killed the wrong person? Should I have lain there, my tongue bloated and black . . . or Melanie?

Flapping. Flapping huge wings. *One of the world's largest condor preserves.* Melanie? Are you still here? Great whooshing sounds as the enormous wings slice into the air. What does a condor look like? Like a griffin? Tired. So tired. *The question isn't one of ownership, but how the hell it got into this room!* Hairy legs. Thumping against a cardboard box. It's moving! Oh my God! It's moving! *Your mother was a woman of enormous endurance. . . . So early in the morning . . .*

❋❖❋

Dr. Adams had let me return to the Musser home four days later. I looked awful. Emaciated, with a sickly pallor that made any attempt at make-up look like a neon light in a black void, and, of course, I was feeble to the point of being unable to walk without assistance. But everyone was so solicitous, so kind, that I sometimes attempted to move about beyond my capacity. Melanie was busy trying to fatten me up with her thick, homemade pea soup, rich with ham hocks and grated carrots. And I don't think I've ever eaten so many fresh vegetable gelatin salads (builds the blood, she'd say). Both Kyle and Juan came to visit daily; Kyle was ebullient, optimistic, and Juan was withdrawn but obviously worried.

About a week later, I made my way downstairs. It was

midafternoon, and while I didn't expect to find William or Alexander, I had anticipated finding Melanie in the kitchen getting the evening supper ready. I was totally unprepared when Ben nearly knocked me down as he stomped from the kitchen into the living room.

"You're up!" He seemed genuinely pleased, an almost embarrassed smile on his lips.

"I couldn't stand staying in bed a moment longer," I responded, noting for the first time how pleasant a face Ben had when he wasn't brooding or scowling. "Where's Melanie?"

He leaned against the wall, not in his usual insolent stance, but just casually. "She hadn't been to market for more than a week," he answered, a light of amusement in his dark brown eyes. "She announced at breakfast today that we were all doomed for certain starvation if one of us didn't take her to town this afternoon."

"How come you didn't get stuck with the job?" I asked kindly, not wishing to upset this "new" Ben I'd just encountered.

He shrugged, his heavy eyebrows forming a gothic arch across his face. "William said he had to order something from the Sears catalogue anyhow. Besides, Butch isn't feeling very well."

"How can you tell when a snake doesn't feel well?" I laughed.

Ben was very serious, though. "They won't eat, for one thing. I've just come from the cellar. Would you like to see it? Get the grand tour?"

I hesitated only for a moment. While I had no real desire to see Ben's chamber of horrors, nonetheless I knew that if I refused, I would make a permanent enemy of him. Perhaps, sharing his keen interest with him, if even for just a few moments, I could get beyond his caustic barrier, his open hostility toward me. My hesitation wasn't lost on him.

"You don't have to go out in the cold," he said softly. "There's a door under the stairs that leads directly to the cellar. And it's quite warm down there. I have to keep it that way, or my pets would die. Most of them, anyway."

His tone of voice, and his facial expression, showed such a

rush of private enthusiasm, I didn't have the heart to say no to Ben. I nodded my acceptance to his invitation, and followed him slowly as he led the way to the door beneath the stairs in the hallway.

Ben preceded me down the rough, wooden plank stairs, extending his almost delicate hand to support me. "Don't put your weight on the railing, it's not safe," he warned me.

When we reached the cellar floor, I was amazed at what I saw. A relatively small room—in comparison to the size of the house—with electric heaters suspended at about every six feet, their warm glow directed downward from the adobe ceiling. Lining each of the four walls were cages made of a heavy mesh-like metal; some looked as if Ben had made them himself, using chicken-coop wiring to keep his creatures enclosed. In the center of the room was a very large wooden table, devoid of any carved adornment, just a sturdy, functional table.

"Here," Ben said, still holding my hand and drawing me toward one of the cages. "Meet Butch."

I approached the cage gingerly. Knowing that they were enclosed, therefore harmless, didn't fill me with any courage. When I reached his pen, he seemed to recoil from *me*, pulling himself into a corner and staring at me intently.

"Isn't he a beauty?" Ben asked with an appreciation for the creature that required no reply.

However, I was forced to admit—reluctantly—that there was a certain kind of beauty to Butch's symmetrical rings and scales. About twenty-five inches long, his body was banded with solid rings of black, broken up with narrower bands of white. The scales were reminiscent of corn on the cob, picked early while the kernels were still petite and succulent. The head, or base of its skull, was only slightly larger than the neck, then tapered to a rounded face, and gently blunt nose. The eyes on each side were wary, but not especially threatening; or perhaps I only thought so because he was captive. "Is he poisonous?" I softly inquired.

"Butch? Oh no! He's a king snake. They don't strike their victims the way a viper does. They're part of the constrictor family, and in this part of the world, one of your best friends. King snakes and rattlers are arch enemies, with the king snake usually the victor."

"Really?" I was awed, quite frankly. That small thing could kill and destroy the horror that had brought Mary's death? "But they seem, well, almost . . . delicate."

"Don't be fooled by that. Butch could crush every bone in your arm if he wanted to."

"What does he eat?" I asked, trying not to let Ben's statement upset me.

"Rodents, mostly. Though if he were still free, he'd also eat small birds if one were unable to fly away. Gophers, insects."

"I see."

"C'mon, let me show you some of the others," Ben said. His delight at having someone to share his world with was obvious in his manner. He dropped terms like *Lampropeltis getulus* and *Sonora semiannulata* the way I might say baking soda and flour. He obviously had an enormous amount of knowledge about snakes, and pointed out to me the differences between the snakes, the way the scales were formed, the iridescent skin and intricate patterns in coloration. Ben rambled on about this snake's rostral, or that one's infralabials; that the scales on the belly are usually larger than on their backs, wider, for certain types of snakes, yet about the same size for other kinds such as the worm snakes. While I couldn't claim to find them attractive as pets, nonetheless I was beginning to lose some of my fear of them.

"Many reptiles are their own worst enemies," Ben said.

"How's that?"

"Being cold-blooded, they seek warmth wherever they can. You'd be amazed at how many snakes are run over on the roads as they try to warm up from the cold nights."

"Isn't that strange," I replied. "You'd think that by now they would have evolved to a more adaptable state."

Ben laughed. "Give them time, they're only two hundred and fifty million years old! And it's the climate, the cold, that killed off most of their ancestors like the dinosaurs."

"But that's what I mean," I insisted, almost forgetting my weakness and illness. "You would think they would have developed some kind of protective warmth against the winters, something which perhaps they would shed during the warmer months."

"Have humans?" Ben countered.

"Well, we're not a two hundred and fifty-million-year-old species. And besides, we invented clothing, fire, electricity . . ."

"We didn't invent fire any more than Columbus discovered America!"

"What do you mean?"

Ben sighed as if having to deal with a retarded child. "Fire has always existed, it's only man's ego to say he 'invented' it; man merely learned to use it at will. Same as with the egomaniacal myth about Columbus. America was already here, the Indians had 'discovered' it long before—Columbus conquered, invaded, whatever you want to call it, but he did not 'discover' the land!"

I found myself looking at Ben in an entirely new way as he explained his views to me. Gone was the sullen, taunting young man. In his place was a serious, knowledgeable person at ease in his own domain and subject. There was a dichotomy about Ben that was strangely fascinating, like his snakes. I said little as he led me to the other cages, smaller ones, where he kept his spiders. Shuddering past the tarantulas, or mygalomorphs, as Ben called them, he told me about the thirty species located in the Southwest, that few were poisonous to man, their molting periods, and much too much to assimilate even had I wanted to. Then on to a corner where the area was darker, and Ben took a flashlight from atop a cage and beamed it into the cages.

"The black widow," he said with pride. "Or *Latrodectus mactans.*"

I stared as one spider seemed to scurry up the web, its shell and legs a glossy black. The other spider had a vivid red marking on what I presumed was its abdomen; it seemed to dig in defiantly.

"The one with the hour-glass red mark is the female. She's the one who builds the nest and you'd be amazed at how strong her strands of silk are."

"I suppose you're going to tell me they're not dangerous either," I joked. It seemed that Ben found nothing dangerous about any of his pets.

"He's not, the black fellow. All the males are concerned

with is finding the female. I've never heard of a case where the male *Latrodectus* has bitten anything, much less a person. See how he's moving about, trying to get away from us? The male's basically a sponger and a coward. But the female is something else again. She'll kill anything she thinks is a threat to her web or her young. Though, if you can get to a doctor fast enough, people don't generally die from the venom—but it's a horrible illness for a while."

"Charming," I said, then hoped he'd not felt I was being sarcastic.

"It's nature. We all survive as best we can, one way or the other," Ben replied simply. "One day, when you're feeling a little stronger, I'll put on a show for you."

"What kind of show?" I asked hesitantly.

"Survival, or as I sometimes call it, my Survivability Games."

"Meaning?"

Ben leaned against the rough table in the middle of the room. "I pit one species against another. Here, on this table. I'll take a cage and, for instance, place a widow with a centipede, or a spitting spider against some other kind. I try to keep the odds even as much as I can. And of course, to watch a king snake crush a rattler is an extraordinary spectacle!"

Glancing at Ben, listening to the aloof, cold tone in his voice, I was once again aware of his almost alien personality. "Isn't that playing a cruel, god-like game?"

He lifted one shoulder as if to say "So what?" then traced an invisible line across the tabletop. "Everything in life has its areas of cruelty. The same thing would happen if they were out on their own in this relentless land. If some other species didn't kill them, the weather would, or a bird would grab them for feed. Nothing lives forever. Nothing should. Life is only a state of transition; we'll all be fertilizing the earth sooner or later."

"Isn't that rather morbid?" I asked softly.

"Just realistic."

"You don't have much respect for life, I gather."

Ben grinned. "As I said, it's a state of existence; being dead is another. In the long run, the cosmic scheme of things, it doesn't matter very much one way or the other."

There was a shield that seemed to clamp behind his eyes as he spoke, as if he were discussing his own emptiness more than anything else, but didn't want me to know. For a few seconds, I let his words hang in the air, let them filter through and settle in our respective psyches. Ben was gazing over my shoulder, his dark eyes changing shades as his dark thoughts roamed through his mind like ghosts in an empty castle. It was a strange moment, a disquieting one. Then, before I knew it was even on my mind, I blurted, "Why do you stay here in Frazier, Ben? Why haven't you moved away to make your own life?"

"Where would I go?" he said quietly. "I'm a misfit. Everyone knows that. Isn't it a shame about Benjamin Musser! Not quite retarded, not quite dangerous, not quite anything."

"But you could change all that!"

"By moving away?"

"Yes," I said with more sternness than conviction. "By getting away from what you seem to believe others think of you. Starting anew, taking pride in being self-supporting. Going to museums, dating . . ."

Ben laughed aloud. "But don't you see," he said, "they're quite right. I know it, so do you. I'm an EMR!"

"What in the world is that?"

"Emotionally retarded. Nothing intrinsically wrong with the intellect, but a case of arrested development psychologically. Who'd want to date *me*?"

"Hello? Anyone down there?"

It was Melanie's voice, calling from the top of the stairs. I was chagrined at her poor timing. Another ten or fifteen minutes and I could have—or at least, might have—broken down Ben's escapist excuses. But the mood was broken instead; the moment had passed.

"Alyce? If you're down there, I'm going to thrash you! You're supposed to be . . ."

"I know, Melanie, I know," I called up to her. "I've only been down here for a little while. Ben's been showing me his collection."

"Alyce Prather Laird, you come upstairs this instant! Can't I leave this house for even five minutes without you behaving like a five-year-old? Land sakes alive, I don't know what to do with either of you!"

I glanced toward Ben, half smiling at Melanie's bawling-out, but Ben's expression had reverted to his usual locked-out vagueness, to a world where no one could enter. Placing my hand on his forearm, I whispered, "We'll talk again, Ben, some other time. I'm sure I can convince you to change your mind."

He glared down at me as if I'd lost control of my senses. "Change my mind? About what?"

"About . . ."

"You'd better go upstairs. I've work to do."

He turned his back on me then, walking toward Butch's cage with shoulders hunched, an aura of preoccupation about his thin body. It was too late to reach him now. Some other time, perhaps—but I rather doubted it.

"Alyce!"

Melanie's voice brooked no nonsense. "Yes, Melanie. I'll be right up." I looked toward Ben just once more. His back was still toward me. It was painful to see what he was doing to himself; how hurt he was in his own world. Yet there was nothing more I could do right then. "We'll talk again," I repeated to him as I started up the stairs.

"Mind the railing," Melanie said, framed in the doorway and frowning. She extended a hand to me as I labored to the top of the stairs, my strength suddenly gone. "What on earth were you doing down there!" she demanded.

I gazed into her worried, round blue eyes and smiled. "Nothing."

CHAPTER FOURTEEN

As the days passed, I grew stronger and was able to spend more and more time out of bed. I saw very little of William and Alexander—and if I saw Ben at all, it was either fleetingly as he turned a corner, or as he wolfed down his evening meal before rushing down to the cellar. He made no reference to that morning in his private world, to our conversation; and much as I really wanted to speak with him again, to try to overcome his resistance to life, I had too much respect for his privacy to bring up the topic without an invitation.

Yet I couldn't bring myself to worry too much about it. Since the day I'd been released from the hospital, and all through my convalescence, Frazier had been basking in an unusual heat wave. The temperature had been in the upper forties and lower fifties, melting most of the snow except where it had reached the deepest drifts, or where it received only a few hours of the early morning sun. Most of the area seemed brown and dead, except for the towering fir trees and other evergreens, yet occasional islands of thick snow patched the terrain like a dab of mayonnaise on a salad that was wilted and listless. But the air was crisp and stung at my nostrils whenever I'd pass by an open window. I longed to be out of doors, to drink in this heady mountain air and let it purge my system of all the germs and staleness of ill health.

My mind kept drifting back to the abandoned mine, and to Kyle's admission about the journal. I'd thus far said nothing about it to anyone, not even Manny. I wasn't quite sure why I was being so secretive; yet something forewarned me, cautioned me to silence. Perhaps it was the over-all attitude at El Fin del Camino; they had all seemed to accept me as a permanent fixture. Nothing was discussed beyond the daily activities—a broken fence post at the lower quadrant, one of the cows seemed off her feed, that sort of thing. Not a word about why I'd come there, nor any reference to when I might depart.

Perhaps it should have struck me as strange, yet it didn't. The Mussers, like so many people in that area, kept their counsel, spoke little, and life seemed to be one of surviving from day to day—there seemed to be no interest in the outside world, in what China was up to, or what the President had just vetoed. They seemed to live in a mirrored room, seeing only what was reflected back with direct involvement. I fell into their microcosmic patterns easily; perhaps due to my illness, perhaps not. Boston seemed eons away; someone else's life, not mine. Or, for that matter, perhaps my acceptance of this new world was based on having a family for the first time; people who were blood relatives, who cared whether I lived or died . . . or at least seemed to. And too, I was so relieved to be regaining my strength that every day was like a minor miracle to me. That my eyes could see filled me with gratitude, that I would awaken feeling even a little bit stronger gave me encouragement. I'd never known serious illness before, and while I hoped I never would again, nonetheless there was a kind of regeneration to the experience. I doubted that I would ever again take my good health for granted, or the gift of life as my due. Regardless of my nebulous acknowledgments to a Higher Power, my illness and recovery had wrought an appreciation for every waking moment I'd not had before.

Wrongdoing, murder, or the past could wait its turn. Regardless of my reasons for coming to California, I was enjoying each minute of my life for the first time, recognizing that no second is like the one before it—and that once past, it could never be recovered.

It was in this frame of mind that I observed Juan Melendez riding toward the house on a broad-chested bay. He had a black, Spanish-brimmed hat on his head, with an Irish-knit white sweater over a blue shirt that was open at the throat. The horse lumbered slowly toward the house the way a large ship rolls with the ocean swells, and Juan rode him easily, confidently. As he drew closer, I could hear the horse's hooves glancing off rocks and see clumps of damp earth tossed as the beast traversed the grassy areas.

From the corner of my eye, I saw Melanie come from the side of the house, wave to Juan, and walk toward him as she wiped her hands on her faded checkered apron. "Well, well," she called, smiling broadly as he brought the horse to a halt before her. "What brings you around these parts?"

He grinned down at her, and, lifting up his sweater, he pulled out an envelope. "It was such a perfect morning, I thought I'd take a ride. Besides, I passed Sam's jeep and he asked me if I'd drop this letter off to Alyce and save him the trip over."

"We're always pleased to see you, Juan," Melanie said. "Alyce's inside. Whyn't you get down and tether your horse, then have some coffee with us," she added.

Juan swung down effortlessly. "Only one cup," he warned. "It's too glorious to be indoors. Maybe Alyce would like to get some fresh air too."

They entered the house noisily, with Melanie carrying on a commentary about my health and progress, and Juan stomping his boots heavily to avoid bringing in any mud. He spotted me at the living-room window, and pulled himself to full height as if he were from the board of health. "A little too pale," he mused aloud. "Too thin, definitely."

I smiled. "Hello, Juan. I heard you say you had a letter for me."

"And here it is," he said, handing it to me with a great flourish.

He smelled of sunshine and leather, and I hoped he would remember to ask me for company on his ride. Clean sheets drying in the sun could smell no sweeter than he did in that musty, damp living room. Glancing at the return address, I saw that it was from Tharon Ann, and knew that it could wait till later to be read, when the mantle of night precluded the activities of the day.

Melanie led the way to the kitchen table, and we drank our

coffee in amiable, idle conversation. Finally, Juan leaned back in the chair and looked longingly out the window. "How's Fury these days?" he asked. "Seem to recall Alexander saying something about her not feeling too well the night of the—square dance," he added slowly, as if sensing our unease at any mention of that night when Mary had died so needlessly.

Melanie and I exchanged covert glances, recalling the original plan for deceiving Juan into visiting me. But Melanie picked up swiftly. "Oh, Fury's been fine, just fine."

Juan nodded with a veterinarian's sage sympathy. "In that case, why don't I saddle him up and take Alyce out for a ride? The fresh air, and the change of scene, would be good for her."

When Melanie said nothing, Juan turned to me. "You do know how to ride, don't you?" he asked, a frown on his darkly handsome face.

"On an English saddle, yes. But I've never ridden Western," I answered, somewhat apologetically.

"Then it's time you do," he said. "A horse is a horse. The length of the stirrup leather is the primary difference; you nearly stand with a Western saddle, no need to post. And, of course, you've the pommel to lean on, if you wish, but it doesn't affect the riding itself. Unless," he said with a teasing smile, "you feel up to roping a calf."

"Well, I don't know," Melanie interrupted. "I'm not so sure Alyce is up to . . ."

"Oh Melanie, please!" I burst out. "I'd so love to get out into the open, to feel myself totally well again. Don't say no!"

She looked across at me, her eyes turning a dark blue with indecision and concern. "If you promise to dress warmly, wear a scarf about your throat . . ."

"I will, I promise!"

"And," turning to Juan, "if you promise to get her back here long before the evening chill sets in. Come three-thirty, four o'clock, it's mighty cold out there."

"I do solemnly swear," Juan said seriously.

To be ruthlessly honest, I bounded from my chair like a teen-ager who has been given a reprieve from punishment. I wasn't going to wait around for Melanie to think of some reason why I couldn't go; so grabbing at Tharon Ann's letter,

I dashed to my room to put on heavier, more suitable clothes. Tossing the letter onto the bureau, I saw Tharon's childlike scrawl in red ink as it landed upside down: Important. Open at once.

Smiling at her typical theatrics, nonetheless I scanned the letter swiftly. She was still concerned about me, it was snowing in Boston, the baby was cuter than ever, and so forth. The aspect of "urgency" lay in the news that she and her husband were going on a two-week holiday, and she wanted me to have a phone number where she could be reached "if you need me for anything." Dear, dramatic Tharon Ann. I began to question whether or not I had been underestimating her affection for me in the past; perhaps my own self-doubts had not permitted me to realize what effect I might have upon others.

But after a moment's musing, I put the letter aside and rushed to change clothes. Now was not the time for such contemplations; now was the time to be with Juan in the clean, fresh air. After all that time convalescing, I desperately needed a change in atmosphere.

❊❖❊

The sun's warm rays and the light breeze as we rode through the uneven, rough forest area coursed through my body like a Jacuzzi bath. I felt alive and vital, and knew by the tiny prickling of my cheeks that a rosy glow was spreading across my face. Fury was, as Melanie had said, a wonderful horse; I had the definite impression that he knew I was no expert equestrienne, and he took all slopes—uphill or down—with exceptional slowness, sensing I'd probably fall off otherwise.

Juan was quiet for the first few miles, as was I. It was indeed a glorious morning, and the smells of the earth reached my nostrils like ambrosia. We rounded a shrub-covered knoll, and there found what was left of an old wooden house. While its builder had provided a foundation to keep the floors off the cold ground, it was a crude structure at best. More than simply abandoned and delapidated, its gray, weathered boards were rough-hewn and no effort had been made to put any kind of border around what used to be the windows.

"This was your mother's home," Juan said gently, breaking our long, enjoyable silence. "She lived here with Sam Musser."

I looked at his quiet, expressionless face, then back toward the house. "But . . . but it's so barren here. There's nothing around for miles and miles!"

Juan nodded. "They liked it that way. They had each other, as my father used to tell me, and the three children."

"The earth doesn't even look like good farmland, little more than shale and grit." I was horrified at this isolated spot, unable to comprehend how my mother could have endured so ugly a place.

"Come," Juan urged, "I'll show you Sam's mine. It's just over there about two hundred yards, behind that slope."

I'd not noticed before that the house was surrounded by hills on three sides; not the steep, mountainous terrain of the Musser ranch, but kinder and softer. I followed Juan in something of a stupor, trying to reconcile the way Manny had described my mother's first marriage with what I'd just seen. A rose garden? In this? No wonder she'd been the marvel of her neighbors! I doubted that even a cactus could grow in such barren soil. A tumbleweed rolled quietly with a sudden gust of chilly wind, and I brought my scarf about my throat in protection. The tumbleweed reached a lumbering sort of momentum as it passed before us, then came to rest at the foot of a gnarled, stumpy tree. It was beyond my comprehension how a few miles could so alter the environment, until I remembered my drive to Frazier. Perhaps we were closer to the freeway now, closer to the town of Frazier itself—which was, indeed, a desolate spot.

As we came around the slope, I saw a gaping hole in the nearby hill. Now the wind carried the sounds of some kind of rattling mechanism, a shifting, grinding sound, and soon I saw a strange structure—rickety at best—with a kind of slide or conveyor from the opening of the mine leading down the eastern portion of the hill beyond our vision. I don't know quite why, but images of Sleepy Hollow and the Headless Horseman came to mind; it seemed a ghostly place for anyone to be.

Of course! I realized suddenly. William still worked his father's mine; this had to be the borax mine Manny had told me about. Even as the recollection came to me, I saw William, covered from head to foot in a grayish powder, ambling from the mouth of the mine. He stopped short, squinted, then waved to us. We rode up to him, but when Juan didn't dismount, I followed his example.

"What brings you two way out here?" he asked, unsuccessfully trying to wipe his chalky hands on his dust-covered clothes.

"We're out for a constitutional," Juan said. "Thought I'd show Alyce where her mother used to live."

"Why not to Horatio's house, then," William drawled. "She'll get the wrong impression from this shack!"

"That's next." Juan laughed.

The unexpected sound of joviality from him caused me to look at him swiftly. I almost gasped aloud as the sun played across his strong, lined face; he was incredibly masculine, like something imagined from the Old West. He sat his mount with pride and dignity, an easy grace in his every gesture. While his features were too rugged, too perfect in their lean planes, I somehow thought he looked rather like a Greek god. There was no doubt in my mind that Juan was his own man, capable of facing anything, or accepting all challenges head-on in successful combat. He was a leader, not a follower; darkly resolute without being offensively aggressive. Juan Melendez was different from any other man I'd ever met before; an enigma that piqued my eastern curiosity. At that precise moment, I wondered if I would ever rest until I understood this man, knew what motivated him, where his thoughts lay. Astride that big bay, the sun's winter warmth upon our faces, I gazed upon Juan as if he were a mountain I should have to conquer, climb to its peak, and plunge my flag by way of territorial imperative.

Feelings I'd never known before flashed through my body. I felt flushed, vibrant, and longed to reach out and touch Juan. It wasn't love. At least, I was relatively confident of that. It was a primitive desire; a physical need to envelop him with a passion I'd never known I could feel. And it was with a combination of heady need and shocking embarrassment that I tore my eyes away from him. In all my thirty years, I'd never before wanted a man. But I wanted Juan, and the knowledge of this carnal aspect brewing within me filled me with sudden shame and tongue-tied guilt.

". . . Don't keep her out too long, Juan," William said, forcing my attention back to the presence of my half brother. I knew I was blushing, but hoped that the rosiness on my face would be attributed to the bracing fresh air.

"I won't," Juan answered, gently pressing the heel of his boot against his horse's ribs. The bay snorted briefly, more from aggravation than discomfort, and slowly walked away, followed obediently by Fury.

"Didn't William want me to see the mine?" I asked, more to get my mind off my new-found physical attraction than from genuine interest.

Juan waited till Fury and I were abreast of him before replying. "There's nothing to see, really," he answered. "These old borax mines are just holes in the ground, supported by beams and crossbeams. William spends his time hammering away at the guts of the mine, dumping the soft rock into the sifter and down the conveyor to his truck. He covers the borax powder every night with a tarpaulin, and when the truck's load is full, he drives it over to Bakersfield. There's nothing interesting or glamorous about it, nothing at all—but you sure would've gotten dirty."

We rode on for a while saying nothing, heading in an easterly direction, which was beginning to look more like the forest again. The sun was directly overhead by then, and Juan reined in at the base of a sharp hill.

"Hungry?"

Actually, my stomach had been grumbling for some time, accustomed as I was to Melanie's force-feeding for the sick. "Ravenously," I replied. "Don't tell me you brought lunch!"

Juan's smile nearly toppled me from the saddle. "I did, such as it is." He dismounted, loosening the bay's cinch before tethering him to a nearby tree.

"Not beef jerky, I hope!"

"No." He laughed, coming over to me and reaching up with one hand to help me dismount. "Just old-fashioned chicken-salad sandwiches, some salami, some cheese, and a nice bottle of local wine."

I brought one leg over the pommel with difficulty, but when I felt Juan's hands about my waist to lift me down, my blood pounded in my veins. I desperately wanted him to hold me closely, my mind a kaleidoscope of old movies on TV where the heroine is knocked from the horse, and the hero takes advantage of the moment to embrace her. Now stop it! I chided myself silently. You're not fourteen years old, and Juan isn't the football star! This adolescent surge of feminine awareness is about as becoming to you as freckles and pigtails! However, I was rather sure that my conscious command would have little effect upon my emergent womanliness.

He led me toward a cluster of boulders jutting from the earth. We climbed some of the smaller ones to those that received the direct sunlight. I was impressed with Juan's agility; he'd not let go of my hand, had a straw picnic basket in the other, and yet clambered up the boulders like a mountain goat. When we reached a flattened area, he set down the basket, blew at the rock's surface to get some of the dust off of it, then gestured to me to sit down.

Juan spread our lunch out, pulling a combination corkscrew and knife from his hip pocket, and proceeded to open the wine. "It's a superb Ridge, vintage, and I think you'll like it."

"I thought all California had was Gallo and Christian Brothers," I said, more to make a comment of any kind since I've never been very familiar with wines.

"No, this is Santa Clara County wine, and I think they are often as good, if not better, than many imported French wines." He poured us each a half glass, and handed one to me. "*Salud, pesetas, y tiempo para disfrutarlas!*"

Well, I'd learned a few things working in the Language Arts Department, and I could say a toast in about seven languages—even if it involved only one word. "*Na zdorovia!*" I replied, and we both laughed.

I pounced on my sandwich with a hearty appetite borne of the clean, rigorous mountain air, and wondered whether he'd made them himself or had a housekeeper. We ate in silence for a little while, taking in the panorama of nature about us until I gestured at a deer that had entered the clearing.

"Shh," Juan admonished. "Don't wave about like that or

you'll frighten it away," he whispered. "It's a doe, foraging for food . . . the stag may not be too far away."

"Are they dangerous?" I asked, keeping my tones as hushed as possible.

"If the stag feels threatened, yes. Just try to hold very still; she'll wander off soon enough . . . there's not much to eat around here at this time of the year. She'd be better off at a higher altitude, where the trees at least provide some foliage."

We watched her together, her graceful neck dipping toward the dead grass in the ground, then glancing at us with eyes so round and brown they were clearly visible even at that distance. Gradually, she started to cross over toward the shrub and trees, and soon she was completely out of sight. If the stag was around, he failed to show up. Straining my neck to catch any possible last glimpse of the beautiful beast, I suddenly noticed what looked like hieroglyphics at the base of our rocks. "What's that?" I asked.

"No one knows for sure," Juan said. "But I thought it might interest you. We've had a couple of archaeologists out to look at them, but all we know is that they're about two hundred years old, and doubtlessly Indian."

I scrambled down the rocks for a closer view. "They look almost like a map," I said, my head about level with Juan's boots.

"Many have thought so. For generations, men have believed that this is the legacy of Tecuya, the last living Indian to know the whereabouts of the fabled mine of the padres."

"The what?"

"A gold mine of such vast wealth and inexhaustible supply that the original Spanish missionaries were able to support Isabella with its wealth, not to mention the Church."

"And no one's ever found it?"

"Not since the old priests. There's a legend about it, naturally, as there is about most mines of untold wealth. Tecuya is said to have died—after almost betraying its whereabouts to the white man who was not a priest—seeing terrible visions, writhing in agony, and taking the secret of its whereabouts with him."

"But this map?"

"Maybe it's a map, or perhaps just an inscription of some kind. The archaeologists don't think it's important enough to try to translate. But Melanie's fiancé died trying to use it as a guide to the mine, and so did Sam Musser. Greed is a very strange thing."

I climbed back up and sat down beside him again. "Then, perhaps this formation of boulders is something like Stonehenge, something to be used in conjunction with the stars and the sun. Has anyone tried to figure if there's a connection?"

"Yes," Juan said slowly, pouring us each a little more wine. "And they too have died. When man prefers to discover wealth, or steal it instead of working for it, he accepts the liabilities which accompany his avarice."

We fell into silence, and Juan carved off some cheese with his knife, then handed it to me. I was filled with questions about this alleged source of great fortune, but managed to keep them to myself. And gradually, the wine began to make me drowsy, and I felt myself becoming mellow with contentment. I leaned back on the smooth surface of the big rock, and let the sun permeate my clothes and relax me even more.

"Alyce," Juan opened, his baritone voice barely heard.

"Um-hm."

"Why did you come to Frazier, come back to this part of the world?"

My eyes opened slowly and I turned on my side, propping my head on my hand. "To meet my relatives," I said slowly, conscious of some greater depth to his question than appeared at first.

"And to find out who killed your father? To claim your share of Kyle's and my fortune?"

His tone was calm, almost casual, but I could feel the tension behind his voice. I could lie to Juan, of course, pretend total ignorance of such a thing. But there are times when one must follow intuition, and mine told me that if I lied to Juan, I would make him an enemy of serious consequence. If I had any chance at all of obtaining his help in finding the journal Kyle had mentioned, my hunch said to be truthful with Juan. My eyes locked with his as I weighed his last question. "If possible," I replied slowly.

He nodded, an expression of weary acceptance crossing his

face. "I thought as much. Thank you for telling me the truth."

"I know about the . . . the journal," I said.

"Yes. Kyle told me he'd revealed its existence to you. It was a very stupid thing to have done."

I propped myself up on my elbow even farther. "Why do you say that?"

Juan rubbed his eyes with his hand. "Because murder somehow always begets yet another murder, or intense emotional suffering that could have been avoided."

"Not necessarily. The truth has never hurt anyone."

"It does," he said softly, "if it jeopardizes someone enough to kill for his secret."

"Would you kill to keep the truth away?"

Juan smiled sadly. "How can I predict what I would or wouldn't do? First I have to feel—"

His answer was cut short by a loud clap in the distance, followed almost at once by a portion of the rock we were on shattering into dust. "Get down!" Juan commanded.

"But . . ."

"Dammit, woman, get down! Someone is trying to kill you!"

CHAPTER FIFTEEN

We crouched behind the boulders for what seemed a
very long time. My limbs were getting stiff from the lack of
circulation, but whenever I made any effort to move, Juan
would glare at me. Ultimately, and I somehow managed to
keep a straight face, Juan removed his hat and placed it on
the neck of the wine bottle; then slowly lifted it above the
boulder—Matt Dillon couldn't have done better.

"It seems to be all right," Juan whispered, holding the hat
aloft still.

I could no longer suppress my amusement and a smile was
bursting to express itself across my face.

"What's so funny?" he asked, his handsome features looking
surprised and worried. "Someone shoots at you, and you think
it's funny?"

"Oh, Juan," I exclaimed, laughter creeping into my voice.
"Just look at us! Like kids playing cowboy and Indians . . .
and you holding up a bottle of vintage wine with your hat on
it, and . . ." I couldn't speak another word and began to
laugh aloud.

Juan stared at me for a moment, then glanced up at his hat
perched askew on the bottle. He brought it down, his own
laughter matching mine, and he set the bottle down on the
earth before he spilled the contents. "So you think it's funny,
do you?" he said, still chuckling at the picture we made.
"Then let's see what you think about this!"

With that, he pulled me to him, his strong tanned hand
cradling my head gently as he softly placed his lips against

mine. His kiss was tender, and he urged my lips apart with knowledgeable, practiced ease. Juan's strong, lean chest pressed lightly against my breast, his other hand gently stroking my face as his lips moved against mine. I felt his ardor in every part of my body and mindlessly entwined my arms about his neck. Instinctively, I arched to be closer to him, to merge with his muscular torso—I felt wanton, heady passion coursing through me, hoping fervently that the kiss would go on forever.

But it didn't. At long last, Juan released me. His breathing was ragged, his eyes somewhat glazed. "Come," he said hoarsely. "I'll take you home."

It was the last thing in the world I wanted him to do; what I wanted, though I couldn't bring myself to admit it openly, was for Juan to take me—all of me. But I sensed that Juan was not the kind of man who would like to be pursued; if there was ever to be any intimacy between us again, he would have to initiate it. Almost meekly, I followed him after we'd gathered up the picnic things and walked back to the horses.

On the ride back, he was quiet, pensive. I couldn't help wondering if he was sorry that he'd kissed me, or if—in my foolish naïveté about such things—I had not been satisfactory as the recipient of his advance. Perhaps a man of his experience expected a different response from a woman; perhaps I should have been a little less open to him, displayed some sort of shock at his boldness. I didn't know how to brook the silence, how to bring Juan back to me.

As we came to the summit of a hillock, El Fin del Camino came into view perhaps a mile or two distant. Juan reined in his bay and Fury took the hint, pawing tiredly at the turf, his breath misting in the beginning of the afternoon chill. Juan turned in his saddle and looked at me with disquiet written across his face, his somber eyes almost black beneath his heavy brows.

"I suppose," he began slowly, "it would be useless to ask you to go back to Boston, to abandon this senseless quest of yours."

Perhaps I became enraged from motives of the proverbial woman scorned, which I felt his remark to indicate, or maybe my stubborn streak was showing as it had when Manny had suggested the same thing. Regardless of why, my indignation was unmistakable. "Quite useless, Juan. I've come a very long way, and gone through too much, to consider quitting now."

"Don't you see what's happening?" Juan demanded in nearly a hiss. "Your presence has already killed an innocent person; Mary Gomez is dead because of you. The tarantula that bit Melanie was meant for you, too. And now you've been shot at. What will it take to make you see that you're a catalyst of death?"

Only the mention of Mary got to me, and for a split second I had to fight back the tears of honest remorse I felt over her senseless demise. Yet Juan's sudden turning on me spurred me to a defensiveness I normally didn't experience. "You're not at all concerned about *me*, but only about those around me!"

I knew it was childish of me the moment the words were uttered, but it was too late to retract them, and Juan's startled scowl forbade swallowing my pride and apologizing.

"I see," he said, his tone disclosing nothing of his real feelings. Instead, he urged his horse forward, breaking into a lope as he headed toward the ranch house.

Fury followed the example, as I longed to call out to Juan, to make him listen to me. To tell him I wasn't really a selfish, spoiled brat . . . more concerned about money than life. But I didn't. I couldn't. My embarrassment and shame were too great for me to admit. I had lived so long within myself that I didn't know how to admit my own stupidity and thoughtlessness. And somehow, these guilty thoughts converted into anger—how *dare* Juan Melendez lead me on with his kiss and then turn on me, telling me to go away before I was responsible for yet another death. Who in the blazes did he think he was! Some Olympian god who was responsible for the world, us mere mortals? By what right did he wish to interfere in what I did or didn't do? As my anger mounted, my resolve to stay on became cemented in my mind. And by the time we reached the house, I was so enraged that I'd convinced myself Juan's only motive could be one of fear: He suspected that it was *his* father who had committed the murder of mine, and he couldn't bring himself to face it. Only the journal held the truth, and I would find that journal if I had to saw down every tree in Los Padres National Forest!

✳︎❖✳︎

"Have a nice ride?" Melanie asked kindly as I stormed into the kitchen, Juan a step or two behind me.

Juan almost collided with me as I stopped dead in my tracks at the sight of Mansfield Watersdown and Kyle Prescott seated at the round kitchen table. "What're you two doing here?" I asked, none too graciously.

Manny smiled slowly. "Beginin' to sound like a Frazier woman . . . got the manners of a horny toad!"

Kyle stood and came toward me, a look of concerned anxiety on his face. "Are you feeling all right?" he inquired. "You look flushed, piqued."

"She should be," Juan intoned in that superior way of his. "She was shot at not more than an hour ago."

Manny half rose from his chair. "What?"

"Shot at! Bang-bang," Juan replied superciliously.

"Where?" Kyle said, drawing me toward the table and pulling out a chair.

"Over toward Morro Flats."

"What makes you think I was the intended victim?" I asked. My question was, obviously, directed at Juan, but I refused to look at him.

"Have you had anything to eat?" Melanie interrupted merrily as if she'd not heard about the shooting. "I spent most of this afternoon in the vegetable patch, but I could rustle up something pretty fast."

"No, thank you, Melanie," Juan said. "We had a light lunch."

"Coffee would be nice," I threw in, mostly to prove my independence from Juan's beatific mantle.

Manny leaned back in his chair, a scowl on his face. "Seems to me that things are getting a little too hot around here. My thinking is that you had best consider leaving this area while the leavin's good."

I bristled at his words; a twenty-mule train couldn't drive me from Frazier at that point in time. If only Juan hadn't kissed me, hadn't made me feel like a desirable woman for the first time in my life—then turn on me like a child. If, if, if—it didn't matter. I was going to find out what really happened to my father; I was going to accomplish what I came here to do. At that precise moment, it wouldn't have surprised me to learn that Juan, at age five, had helped his father murder mine!

Manny clucked irritably. "You've got that Prather look on your face, Alyce. I can see that trying to talk some sense into you would be like trying to stop a mudslide with a siftin' pan!"

"That's right," I answered, but I was beginning to relent in my angry stubbornness. Certainly, I planned to stay on until the issue was resolved once and for all; but my defensive hostility was abating.

Melanie placed a steaming mug of coffee before me, and brought the old ashtray from the countertop. She seated herself with a wistful smile on her face. "That's silly, Manny. You can't stop *any*thing with a sifting pan!"

Her inane response eased the tension in the room considerably, but I was sorry that she was going through one of her lapses again. She'd been doing so very well recently, paying attention, and able to follow a conversation without drifting off to her own private world. Obviously, she'd totally forgotten how angry she'd been with Manny while I was still in the hospital; though I would have preferred to believe she'd simply forgiven him. And much as I hated to attribute Ben's instability to growing up in Melanie's company . . . it seemed quite unavoidable.

I sipped the scalding coffee carefully, waiting for someone to say something to break the ensuing silence following Melanie's remark.

Finally, Juan spoke up: "Did you two come over here together?" His tone was casual; almost too much so.

"No. Why?" Manny replied. "I got here shortly after Kyle telephoned me at the cabin. He told me about the journal—"

"He *what!*" Juan was livid.

"The journal," Manny answered evenly. "I agreed to meet him here at three."

"And just why would you tell Manny about it after all these years?" Juan sounded weary.

Kyle ran his fingers through his thick blond hair. "I saw no reason not to. Alyce already knew. . . ."

"Only because, again, *you* told her."

"Well, I think Kyle's right," Manny interjected. "Let's get to the bottom of this thing once and for all. This mystery's been hangin' over us all like a belch that won't come up, and it's time to end all the speculation and the gossip!"

"C'mon, Juan," Kyle solicited. "The pact we made was when we were just kids. Surely you can see the logic of unearthing the truth after all these years. What possible harm can it do? Even if the journal says that one of our fathers was a murderer—or for that matter, maybe they pulled it off together—that doesn't make *us* guilty."

Juan's sneer was filled with disgust. "I see. And if it turns out that it's your father? That mine had nothing to do with it? What then! Do you plan to give Alyce her share of the mine's earnings over the past thirty years?"

"More coffee, Alyce dear?"

Juan shook his head at Melanie, indicating that this was not the moment for such things. She twinkled sweetly at him, folding her hands before her, her head following from one to the other of us.

"There's more than enough to share," Kyle said, though somewhat sullenly. "And why should it be my father any more than yours? Better it should be yours," Kyle said with a light laugh. "At least you've got an established practice to tide you over."

"I don't give a damn about the money and never have! You know that perfectly well! But you *do!* You've got nothing to fall back on, nothing you can do to actually earn a living—and, being the *bon vivant* that you are, coughing up that kind of cash would break your heart!"

"What are you suggesting?" Manny interfered.

"I'm saying that I think this sudden attitude of co-operation from Kyle is a crock! I think it's a ruse to throw suspicion off himself."

There was a deadly silence for a few seconds. Kyle's fists clenched and pressed hard upon the table as if it were the only way he could avoid lashing out at Juan. "What suspicion?" he asked steadily.

Juan's face was a mask of tense accusation, and his voice was charged with conviction. "You were the last one to arrive at the square dance. You could've pretended to be drunk—

which no one would think unusual—and shown up after placing that Diamondback rattler in the porch while Alyce was still in the kitchen. It certainly would account for your strange behavior when you found her in the barn instead of where you'd last seen her!"

Kyle's mouth had tightened into a white line, his light blue eyes turning a veiled, slate color. "Go on."

"Where were you this afternoon about one o'clock? You happen to be a very good marksman, Kyle. Just not quite good enough—it was a marginal miss," Juan said, his eyes narrowed and his perfect hands spread palms downward on the tabletop.

"I suppose I put the tarantula in Melanie's bedroom," Kyle snarled. "Then I saved Alyce's life at the mine so I could take my time in murdering her. You're an ass, Juan, a first-rate jealous idiot! You've spent your whole life in this rotten place, putting on the act of the rich kid who doesn't let it go to his head. A vet! Is there anyone in the world who doesn't love veterinarians? Kind to God's wee creatures and all that nonsense! Sure I like to travel, and I always will. I like good booze, good food, and bad women—you're damned right I do! I've never had any reason not to! But I'm not a liar, a cheat, or a phony like you!"

"Gentlemen, gentlemen!" Manny said, holding up his hands in protest. "This is getting us nowhere!"

"Where were you about one o'clock?" Juan repeated, ignoring Kyle's accusations.

Kyle's hands unclenched and a small smile crept across his face. "I was on the phone with Mansfield Watersdown," he said calmly.

Juan lurched to his feet. "Is that true?" he hurled at Manny.

The old lawyer's head cocked to one side. "Can't say for absolute certain," he drawled. "It was around then, I suppose, but you know I don't bother with clocks at the cabin."

"We've an extra one upstairs, Manny," Melanie said brightly. "Be glad to lend it to you."

The fury on Juan's face would have backed off an advancing army. "All right, Kyle, have it your own way. You go ahead and search for the journal, put on your show of the knight in shining armor. But I'll tell you something right now.

I do not intend to help you, and if you find a journal that says it was *my* father . . . it better be a diary that can sustain authentication of its age! This game of yours, this sudden switch, is just a little too damned pat!"

And with those words, Juan strode from the room with such anger that the floorboards vibrated with the violence of his footsteps. Then the front door slammed.

Needless to say, I was depleted. Emotionally drained and what little bit of strength I thought I'd regained in the recent days evaporated with the heated scene I had just witnessed. Dusk was rapidly approaching, and I felt there was a symbolic justice to it: nature was bringing the curtain down on the violence of mankind, the mistrust, the frailty, and the fear. I wanted to go to my room, to lie down and try to pull my conflicting thoughts together.

If my life was truly in jeopardy, then why was it so difficult to get rid of me? Kyle couldn't be the culprit for the simple reason that he needn't have "found" me at the mine; he could easily have just let me freeze to death out in the snowstorm. Or, my jumbled mind tried to reason, perhaps that would have been too obvious; maybe he did intend to save my death for a moment when he'd have a better alibi. It couldn't be Juan who wanted me out of the way; he was with me when the shot was fired, narrowly missing his own death if the bullet had gone a scant few inches awry. Yet . . . Juan had come up *behind* me at the barn that horrible night. He was not inside with the others; he could've placed the snake on the trash can in the back porch.

And then, a terrible thought entered my overwrought mind: What if Juan and Kyle were conspiring? What if their argument was merely a ruse? What if . . .

"Well," Manny dragged out slowly, breaking my introspective meanderings, "if you're not goin' to invite me to stay to supper, I'd best be getting along."

Melanie shook her head with irritated disbelief. "Why, Manny, of *course* you'll stay to supper! You too, Kyle. With all that arguin' and shoutin', my mind just plumb didn't think of askin' you all. I just get so addled when people are shoutin' at one another."

With that, she rose from her chair and crossed over to the

refrigerator, opening it wide and perusing its contents with absorbed concentration. Manny got up and poured himself a cup of coffee, looking over Melanie's shoulder with obvious anticipation at the notion of a "good hot meal."

"C'mon," Kyle said with a heavy sigh. "Let's go outside and unsaddle Fury. You can help me."

His gaze was unflinching, his previous anger gone. He seemed a small boy, exhausted after a grueling contact sport. As I looked into his face, I knew that Kyle could never kill anyone. He was spoiled, self-indulgent—but he was no murderer.

I rose from my chair, still feeling weak from the previous tension, and Kyle handed me the shawl from the peg near the door. As I wrapped it about my shoulders, he opened the dining-room doorway that led to the courtyard, and waited for me, a sad, almost regretful expression on his face. "I want to talk to you," he said. "Alone."

✳✿✳

The first few stars could be seen faintly as the sun lowered behind the mountains, a dark, burnt orange color as if it resented having to abandon its domain. To the east, a three-quarter moon was gathering its luster, gloating over the retreating sun. The brief warmth of the day was now abandoning us, and I pulled the shawl about my shoulders to ward off the winter evening's cold. Strange, I thought, how calmly routine everything in life was, with the exception of human calumny. Everything about the universe, about the earth itself, abided by the ebb and flux of existence. It seemed that everything had a timetable, a schedule that could not be broken. Winter "gives" to spring; the sun makes way for the moon—there's no argument about it, no wars fought. Florae bear their leaves and buds, they live, and then they die; no remorse, no useless insistence about the unfairness of it all.

And it seemed to me, at that moment as I followed Kyle toward the barn, that humans were a foolish lot. What possible difference could it make to know the truth about my father. Would it bring him back? Would it return to my mother the life that she wasted? Would I be a better person for the knowledge? And yet, I knew that I would not give up the search. Whether one wished to call it God-given, or evolution, the point remained that I was a creature of reason. I was not a planet or a tree; I was a rational and emotional individual—influenced by my surroundings, but not dominated by them. I wanted to learn the truth; that it would mean nothing to anyone else a hundred years from that moment was irrelevant. It meant something to *me;* and for whom else did I lead my life? No one else would lie in my grave when I died; no one else would have to make an accounting for my behavior. I could not live my life by proxy; I was responsible for and to myself, and to myself alone. Having been raised to believe in justice, in honesty and decency—I had no choice. Not if I wanted to be at peace within myself for the rest of my days.

Juan and Manny wanted me to abandon the mystery, let things be. But to do so would be to deny my own sense of self. I did not believe that I was a catalyst for death, as Juan had said. The guilty always find ways of harming the innocent. I was prepared to concede that perhaps my presence was hastening matters—but that was all. Manny's attitude of letting sleeping dogs lie was all very neat and logical on the surface; but dogs do not sleep forever, whether you awaken them or not. No. I was doing what I knew had to be done, and I could not permit myself to be dissuaded by the concepts of others.

"You look a million light-years away," Kyle said.

I was startled by the sound of his voice and laughed somewhat nervously. "I was," I answered. He had already loosened the cinch of Fury's saddle, and I briefly wondered if Fury was glad or not.

"Here," Kyle said. "Hold the reins while I get this off."

I moved to Fury's nose, took the reins loosely in my hand, and rested my face against the warm, soft cheek of the beast. "I feel as if I've been put through a meat grinder," I said.

Kyle laughed. "You have. And besides, I think you may be in a state of shock over that shooting today. Could there be any chance the shot came from a hunter, a lousy marksman?"

Fury snorted gently, then whinnied. "I don't know," I said. "There had been a doe in the clearing just moments before."

Kyle nodded. "Not an impossibility, then."

He removed the heavy, tooled-leather Western saddle from Fury's back, and lugged it toward the barn. I followed, leading Fury behind me, who was then nuzzling at my neck. Kyle placed the saddle on its stand, then took Fury's reins from me and led him to his stall, removing the bit carefully, and rubbing his nose affectionately. Then he turned and faced me, a clouded, serious look on his face. "There's something I want to explain to you, Alyce."

I looked into his eyes and saw they were guarded, belying his casual stance. It seemed better to say nothing, to wait for him to go on.

"What I said, inside, during the argument with Juan . . . about, about liking 'bad women.' It was true. I mean, it *was* true—it's not anymore." He glanced away from me, then ran his fingers through his hair. "Up in the mine that night of the blizzard . . . I realized something. I learned that so much of my carousing has been due to not wanting to face life—the facts, if you prefer. I breezed through school, had plenty of money, and never wanted to know the truth about your father's death. I guess you'd say I was trying to escape."

"That's understandable," I said, almost inaudibly.

"No, let me finish. When things come easily to you, you take them for granted. And when a man refuses to look at things, well, there's nothing to decide about, is there? So that's one reason why I've changed my mind about helping you."

"Do you need another reason?" I asked.

"It doesn't matter," Kyle said with a slight shrug. "I have another anyway. It's you."

"Me?"

He grinned then. "Yes. I've never known a woman like you. You've got courage, Alyce, courage and grit and stamina. You're intelligent, and you've a good sense of humor. You're a fine woman, and . . . well, I've fallen in love with you!"

"Oh Kyle," I said, instinctively placing my hand on his arm.

"No, now look. I know I've made a mess of my life thus far. I couldn't earn a living if I had to, and I drink enough to sustain the economy of Scotland. But it doesn't have to be that way, Alyce—not if I had someone like you to stand by me while I straightened myself out."

"But . . ."

"I don't expect you to answer me now. Not for quite some time, actually. You don't really know me, what I'm really like.

I've been drunk for so long, I don't think I even know myself. But if I could prove myself to you, Alyce, show you that I am worthy of your love . . . Oh hell, that sounds so damned Victorian! But I mean it. I want you to give me some time to get myself redirected, to become the kind of man you'd want for a husband. You'd make me very happy. I already have the motivation, I just need your patience and understanding."

I didn't know what to say or how to react. I was more than flattered, yet so taken by surprise that I didn't know what to do.

Kyle stepped toward me, placing his hands on my arms, then leaned down and gently kissed me on the forehead. "No promises from you right now. Think about it, that's all I ask. And tomorrow morning, I'll be by for you. We can comb through my house all day to see if we can find that damned journal. All right?"

He placed his arm about my shoulder and we began to walk back toward the house just as William's battered old Ford pulled up next to Manny's four-wheeler. He waved to us, and in the distance I could just make out Alexander coming in from the pasture. The lights had been turned on in the house, their yellow glow beckoning from the windows. The house seemed warm, comfortable; and the men were coming in from their day's labor.

I felt at home. A sense of security and family ties, of people who cared about me and wanted what was best for me.

Tomorrow we would search for the journal. But that was tomorrow. Right then, I knew only a sense of belonging, and that I had just received my first genuine marriage proposal. It had been quite a day!

CHAPTER SIXTEEN

Kyle's home was not at all what I had expected. It was rustic, made from enormous logs with mortar oozing between them. Set into the mountainside, surrounded by giant firs and pines, I had no idea how large it was until we were inside it. It was built on three levels, with a small attic or studio perched off to one side.

The interior was totally masculine, with hunting trophies suspended wherever there was enough space. The furniture, though old, was serviceable and in sturdy good taste; no spindly Louis XIV chairs, but solid and comfortable and built to last. There were two bedrooms on the main floor; the kitchen and living room were downstairs. The third floor housed the master bedroom—which was huge—the bathroom off it, and a narrow winding staircase that led to the attic.

"I had expected opulence," I said as we finished taking a tour of the house. "Grand antiques and crystal chandeliers."

Kyle laughed. "'Fraid not," he said, then sobered and added, "I was a breech birth—and it killed my mother. So just my dad and I lived here until he died from a stroke seven years ago."

"You must've been terribly lonely in this enormous house, all alone."

"Not really. I have never spent that much time around Frazier—no reason to. This house has always been a mood to me, an atmosphere. I go away, and when I'm bored with what I'm doing or the set I'm traveling with . . . I get the mood to come here and hole in."

I smiled slowly. "But then you get bored with being here. . . ."

"Right. And I go on a drunk. And I go away again. Pretty stupid, isn't it?"

"Not for an escapist, it isn't." I laughed.

Kyle pursed his lips and, feigning a naughty schoolboy's look, nodded his admission of wrongdoing. "C'mon, let's get cracking."

We began in the attic, which was more like an office or den, with a huge oak desk, swivel chair, and old-fashioned glass-enclosed oak bookcases. On the opposite side of the room, a badly torn leather sofa squatted beneath two windows that afforded a magnificent view of Mount Pinos in the distance. "Any hidden passageways or secret panels?" I asked.

"Not that I've ever known about," Kyle answered. "But then, I've never looked."

"I'm beginning to feel like Nancy Drew." I laughed. "We must look for innocent panels that, when pushed, lead to damp, hidden chambers."

"Not likely," Kyle said. "If you'd known my father, you'd know he'd never go in for that type of thing. He was raised as a Fundamentalist, and while he never went to church, he never outgrew his religion. He used this room to keep his books, his ledgers, from the mine. A bookkeeper by trade before the mine began to pay off, everything in his world was organized, easily catalogued, and dull as all blazes."

"Did you love him very much?"

"I suppose so. I never thought about it. He wasn't an affectionate man, at least not openly. Dad had his work, and his duty to his only son. We got along nicely, and he'd often take me hunting with him. But we didn't speak a lot. Just a comfortable companionship."

Kyle began pulling the drawers out of the desk, peering inside the cavities as though the diary might be taped to the underside. "Aren't you going to look inside the drawers?" I asked.

He shook his head. "I've been using this desk for the last seven years, I'd have found it if it were that visible." Satisfied that there was nothing concealed within the desk, he replaced the drawers. "Why don't you start digging into the closets, I'll tackle the bookcases."

I nodded and crossed the room toward a small closet, and opened the door. Ordinarily, I'd have felt like an intruder, violating the privacy of others; but Kyle's attitude precluded such an attitude. His enthusiasm was catching, and I felt as if we were conspirators in a common cause.

We went through every room in that house with painstaking care; feeling window ledges, checking for loose floorboards, moving furniture about to look behind it or under it, and even tapping the walls for hollow sounds. With the exception of breaking for lunch, two TV dinners hastily prepared by Kyle and wolfed down, we didn't let up in our search even for a coffee break. We even checked the rocks in the walk-in fireplace in case one of them was loose, easily removed for a concealing place. Nothing. Not one single spot where anything could possibly be hidden went unchecked; and we came up empty-handed.

Tired, covered with dust, we collapsed in the living room just as the sun was setting. "What about the barn or garage," I said, splayed ungracefully in the armchair, my jeans looking as if they'd gone through the Revolutionary War and my cream-colored sweater a rumpled mess.

"We don't have either, never did."

"Would your father have buried it somewhere? Out in the yard or someplace?"

"Not likely. If a man keeps a diary, he's not going to go out and dig it up every day to make a new entry."

I sighed heavily. "What if he was hiding it, finished with it, and not wanting anyone to ever find it?"

Slowly, Kyle shook his head. "I told you, he died from a stroke. It was a sudden and unexpected death." He rose up wearily from the couch, his hands upon his knees for impetus. "No, Alyce, the journal simply isn't here."

He crossed over to the hutch at the far end of the room. "I don't know about you, but I could use a drink."

"Under the circumstances, I'll join you . . . but a weak one, please."

"You're not going to bawl me out for falling back into my old patterns," he said with a surprised look on his face.

"There's nothing wrong with a drink now and then," I replied evenly. "It's excessive drinking that's wrecking your life." I felt an awful knot of tension forming in the pit of my stomach; not because of Kyle's drinking, but because we couldn't find the diary in his house. If it wasn't at this house . . . it had to be at Juan's. I didn't want the diary to be at Juan's house. Somehow, if Kyle's father had been the culprit, I had the impression that Kyle would be able to adjust to the information. I kept recalling Juan's expression the evening before, when he'd so vehemently insisted that any diary condemning his own father would have to be authenticated. I was convinced that Juan would take it very badly, and I wished that we could somehow spare him the humiliation, the shame of it.

Kyle handed me the amber drink, touched my hair lightly, then returned to the well-worn divan across from me. "You realize what this means, don't you?"

The pungent odor of the drink made me wince, but I sipped at it anyway. I really didn't want to articulate what the results of the day meant; as if by saying it, it was so. Juan was such a proud man, so determined to be his own person; I hated the thought of what lay in store for him.

"It means," Kyle went on, "that we'll have to somehow break into Juan's house. He certainly isn't going to just let us in!"

"But we can't do that!" I blurted.

"We'll have to," Kyle said softly, "unless you want to forget about the whole thing."

For a second, I was tempted. I had visions of Juan collapsing with the information, moving away to some strange place, giving up his veterinary practice where everyone had known him all his life. My indecision must have shown clearly on my face. Kyle had risen to his feet to come to me, kneeling down before me, and cupping my face in his broad, strong hands.

"Honey," he whispered. "What Juan's father may have done isn't a reflection on him. He's not going to be tarred and feathered, or treated shabbily by the people of Frazier."

I couldn't help the tears that began to form in my eyes. "Oh, Kyle! He's so terribly proud!"

"Would you prefer to have found it here? Don't you think I'd have a serious reaction, too?"

Yet, I kept remembering Juan as we sat on that boulder having our picnic lunch, which he had so thoughtfully brought along. His rugged handsomeness . . . his kiss that had given rise to feelings I had never known. And I remembered my saying that the truth had never hurt anyone; and his reply: "It does, if it jeopardizes someone enough to kill for his secret."

Would Juan kill to keep the truth at bay? I didn't know; I didn't want to know.

"Darling," Kyle said, bringing my attention back to him. "Do you want to drop the whole thing? I think we've gone too far to let it go now, but if you want to—"

Suddenly, Kyle's face contorted strangely, and he grabbed at his stomach as if being stabbed with terrible pains.

"What's wrong?" I demanded, all other thoughts flying from my mind.

"The drink," Kyle rasped. "There's something in . . . in the drink!" He fell to the floor, rolling up into a fetal position, and I could see spasms of agony in his eyes.

"I'll—I'll call Doc Adams," I said, confused and terrified by Kyle's suffering.

✳◦✳

The doctor had come with a paramedic squad, and in moments had stretched Kyle in bed in the master bedroom and pumped his stomach. I stayed with him through the night, seated at his bedside in case he awoke and needed anything, and Doc Adams took the bottle of scotch with him to have it analyzed.

In the morning, Kyle was feeling infinitely better, but was still too weak to get up from bed. About eight-thirty, the doctor telephoned. "Rat poison," he said simply.

"But how? I drank the same scotch, from the same bottle!" I glanced at Kyle as he listened to my side of the conversation.

He waved to me to interrupt Doc Adams. "Yours was practically water, on the rocks, mine was the straight stuff."

"I don't know how, much less why," Doc Adams resumed. "But someone poured it into the bottle, and it could've killed him if you hadn't been there to call me."

In a shocked daze, I thanked the doctor and hung up, then told Kyle what he'd said. "That does it, Alyce," he said. "Things have to come out into the open now. There's no turning back until we have the truth. Thus far, I've been willing to believe that everything that's happened could just as easily be accidental as deliberate. But not now."

"You think Juan . . ." I couldn't finish the sentence.

"What else can I think? If he truly has believed all these years that his father was a murderer, if he's grown up with some kind of twisted guilt about it, then it's quite conceivable that he'd do anything to stop us from finding that diary!"

"But he was with me when that shooting occurred!"

"And it could've been nothing more than a hunting accident, purely coincidental to everything else that's happened. No, Alyce, I think it's pretty obvious that Juan just isn't quite right in the head. He *couldn't* be, if he's willing to go to such lengths to protect the memory of his father!"

There was nothing I could say. Nothing. I felt empty, sick to my very marrow. Dashing Juan, the Greek god who was really a Mexican—I just could not bring myself to accept what Kyle was alleging, and yet there was no other explanation.

Kyle's hand covered mine. "Go on home, darling, get some rest. I'll be up in a day or two, and then we can think of some ploy to get Juan out of town or something. You're not fully recovered yourself yet, and this has been an awful shock for you."

He was right, of course. My mind was a maze of contradictory thoughts, and my emotions were like opposing armies scrambling to take the same hill. It was impossible for me to think lucidly, and my pulse was racing. I slumped in resignation, then extricated my hand from Kyle's and slowly stood up. My legs felt unsteady and I longed for the quiet comfort of my own room at El Fin del Camino. For some of Melanie's home cooking, the warmth of a kitchen with delicious aromas drifting to the nostrils; to peace and serenity. "I'll have to use your car," I said at last, my tiredness evident in my voice.

Kyle smiled reassuringly at me. "Then you'll just have to drive it back tomorrow when you come for me. I'm sure I'll be all right by then, and we can sit down and map out a plan of action." He paused, his blue eyes gazing intently into my own. "I'll miss you," he said softly.

He smiled feebly as I left his room and made my way downstairs and out to his car. I saw nothing as I drove back to the house; and felt nothing but stupor.

Unless Kyle had poisoned his own bottle, knowing that I would be there to save his life . . . but no. That was too ludicrous. We'd searched for the diary and I was satisfied it wasn't there. But what if Kyle had already found it, and destroyed it—why not let me search his house then? But if that were the case, then why should he bother to go through poisoning himself? It was all so terribly complicated and convoluted.

And I knew then that I'd have to stop to see Manny first, to let him know what had happened, and get his best thinking. I couldn't go back to the house without some sort of objective opinion, from someone who wouldn't care who was guilty and who was not. Manny would think of something I'd overlooked; he *had* to! I couldn't bear the idea of Juan's guilt.

✳❖✳

"Well, of course," Manny drawled out slowly, "Juan could be schizoid."

"What?"

"Schizoid. Split personality." His old hands trembled as he tried to light his pipe, seated in his favorite armchair.

"You mean not know what he's doing?" My mind flashed vivid courtroom scenes, pleading insanity for Juan, getting him carted off to some mental institution. The picture was too real, too horrible to sustain. Not Juan! Some stranger one reads about in a newspaper, yes; but not Juan!

"Mind you," Manny said, "I've never known a more level-headed lad in these parts, but I'm not a psychiatrist."

"I don't believe it," I answered.

"You don't have to. A jury does."

My hands gripped the familiar coffee mug as my mind wrestled with the possibility. I felt as if I'd not slept in months instead of just one night, but my body refused to stop running, to slow down and get some rest. Things were too close to a head, too near to resolution. I didn't dare let up at this point. I couldn't possibly sleep, not knowing if Juan was a murderer or insane, or both; and I cursed myself silently for ever embarking on this voyage of terror.

"There's only one thing to do," Manny said, interrupting my mental diatribe. "And that's to follow out Kyle's plan of searching Juan's house."

"How?"

"It's been made a lot simpler than you two had thought," Manny chuckled. "You call up Melanie now and tell her you're here, and that you're staying to supper. I'll phone Alexander soon as we've had something to eat and explain what we're up to so they don't worry about you."

"But . . . but Juan!"

"Juan, m'girl, is over at the Weiler ranch trying to coax a stubborn horse to give birth to her first foal! He'll be there at least until later tonight, and with any luck at all, probably the whole night! We'll have the house to ourselves, with no interruptions!" Manny was gleefully pleased with himself.

"And what if he isn't? What if the mare is delivering her foal right this second and Juan is back before nightfall?"

"Then we don't go in, that's all." Manny puffed on his pipe smugly. "So, first things first, you get Melanie on the line, and then you're to lie down till supper. Don't want you dead on your feet while we're trying to locate the journal!"

I stared at him blankly. There was something wrong with the scheme. I could feel it. Gooseflesh crept up my arms as negative, anxious vibrations coursed through me. It was too simple; and too soon. I wasn't ready for such swift action, such an unexpected twist of events. "Manny," I said, then hesitated uncertainly.

"Face it, Alyce! If Juan is a killer, he must be stopped. We don't have enough to go on to call in the sheriff, so it has to be done this way. Might be kinder for Juan all the way 'round this way. We'll find the journal, and once we know what's in it, we can confront him as a united block—but of friends, not the police. I'm sure he'll see reason at that point—he's a bright fellow, and if I show him an avenue for defense, I don't think he'll give us a hard time."

"But . . ."

"It's got to be done, Alyce. When we have the evidence, an

actual motive for attempting to kill you and Kyle—who turned coat by helping you—then we can do what's right and best for Juan."

"Shouldn't Kyle be with us?" I was frantically searching for a way to postpone the inevitable.

"No, Alyce. We don't need Kyle to search the house, and with Juan away right now, it's perfect timing. And once we know the truth, face Juan with it, if Kyle were there it could trigger Juan into God knows what! Best leave Kyle out of this until the entire matter is done and over."

I mulled his words over for a few seconds. "Does finding the journal, even if it says that Mr. Melendez was a killer, does that prove that Juan is too?"

Manny clucked in irritation. "It gives us a motive. Mary Gomez is dead, Kyle might have been, and your life has—at least on circumstantial evidence—been jeopardized as well. Who else would care, Alyce? Who else has a motive to kill except someone who has a maniacal desire to keep the truth undiscovered? If Kyle isn't guilty, and we've no reason to assume that he is, then there's only one person left who stands to gain by preventing you from finding that diary. Juan Melendez!"

The silence that followed was as heavy as molasses on a soufflé. With a leaden heart and wooden legs, I rose and crossed to Manny's telephone, then dialed Melanie.

CHAPTER SEVENTEEN

We rounded a steep curve in the four-wheeler, then Manny pulled over to the soft shoulder of the road and turned off the headlights. "We'll sit here a few moments till my eyes get used to seeing by moonlight," he said over the idling engine.

"Are we close to his house?" I wasn't sure quite why, but we were both speaking in husky whispers, as if Juan might overhear us.

Manny nodded. "There's a dirt road turnoff about half a mile up. Leads straight to Juan's cabin. If his car's there, we turn around and think of something else by way of gettin' inside his place."

"Tonight?"

"No. Some other time. But if his car's not there, we go in."

He sounded a little like a general talking to his staff about taking an enemy stronghold. I was, as might be expected, unashamedly terrified. Actually to break into someone's home, to rummage through someone else's personal belongings . . . the furtiveness, the secrecy, and the fear of what we might discover, all left me quivering internally. My stomach was in knots, and my hands—despite the kid gloves I wore—were cold and clammy. My temples were literally throbbing with tension. My face felt flushed, feverish despite the winter chill in the night air; I hoped I was not risking a relapse with pneumonia. I shivered.

"You all right?" Manny asked.

I smiled feebly. "Yes. Just a chill."

Manny peered at me intently, and the moonlight threw eerie shadows across his face, giving him a sinister, malevolent look; his glistening brown eyes, so deeply set in his head, seemed more like the obsidian threat of the rattler's than human. I knew my imagination was running amok, that old Mansfield Watersdown was my friend, still. . . . It took sheer will power to bring my thoughts under control, to remind myself that it was the situation, not the man, that was frightening me so. Then Manny put the car into first gear. "We can go on now," he said softly. "I'll watch the road, you keep a sharp eye out the rear. Don't want any cars ramming us 'cause we've no lights."

Creeping slowly forward, it seemed an endless drive till we turned off onto the dirt road. Even with the moonlight, I could dimly make out what could only be a mountain cabin, situated about one hundred yards ahead. We were nearly upon the house when I spotted a light on in the rear. "Manny!"

"Yep, I see it too. Doesn't mean anything. Juan always leaves a light on in his den. He's got an old cat, and she can't see too well anymore."

"Are his offices here, too?"

Manny shook his head. "No. They're in town. The cabin's too remote." He held up his hand to silence me, then leaned forward, straining to see through the windshield. "There's the garage. See a car?"

"No. It's empty."

"Then I'll park 'round behind it so no one can see us from the road. I'm a tad too old to spend the rest of my days in the pokey for breaking and entering."

"Manny," I said hesitantly. My nerves felt like exposed circuitry.

He laughed lightly. "Now, don't you worry. We'll not get caught. I promise you that."

He pulled up behind the garage and switched off the ignition. The silence was ear-shattering, and my heart pounded in my breast. Manny opened his door quietly and gestured to me to do the same. Once outside the car, and away from its heater, the cold night seemed hostile and forbidding. Neither of us closed the doors all the way, as if the noise would give away our presence; though who would hear us, I couldn't imagine. Manny held my hand as we crept toward the small cabin. It wasn't much larger than Manny's, actually, which surprised me. Our shoes made crunching sounds as we crossed over, leaves and gravel giving way to our progress. As the front door loomed ever closer, I'd have given anything to be back in my own bed; back in Boston, for that matter. Anywhere but here, in the middle of a forest somewhere out in California, on a fool's errand which might end up getting us both imprisoned or killed. Silently, I called myself every kind of idiot known to mankind. Why, why, had I *ever* come to this desolate area? I could have gone to Europe on a sabbatical to grieve my mother's loss, or taken a course in macramé to occupy my hands and mind. But no. I'd come to Frazier instead. It was too late, I knew. Whatever happened next, regardless of the consequences, I'd brought it on myself.

Manny tested the front-door latch. It lifted up easily, and the door swung open effortlessly. He urged me to precede him, and I stepped up into the living room with almost paralyzing trepidation. The light from the den filtered into the living room, but Manny pulled a large flashlight from his hip pocket and beamed it about the room, a scowling intent on his face.

I fervently wished that Kyle were with us. That we were vulnerable was the understatement of the century! An eighty-nine-year-old man, and a sickly, underweight woman, stealthily searching someone's home in the night. What if Juan were to come in at that moment? What if, in the darkness, he thought we were burglars and fired at us? Which, my mind replied with cool logic, he'd be entitled to do; we *were* in his house to steal something.

There was something wrong. I could feel it. An aura of things not being quite as they should; although I'd never been in Juan's house before, I sensed it was somehow "different." Tentacles of terror crept up my spine, fanning out through my body in rigid foreboding. Someone else was in that house. Someone who was expecting us. Waiting. Just waiting.

I began to perspire freely, my hands trembling with this awareness. Just as I reached out to touch Manny's arm, to somehow mime my apprehensive conviction to him, the voice broke the horrible silence.

"I'm right sorry you two are here. I'd hoped this wouldn't be necessary."

Manny whirled with his flashlight in the direction of the voice. Though it wasn't really necessary. We both knew who it was; the voice was easily recognized.

Even as the beam reached her, Melanie threw on the light switch and negated the blinding effect of the flashlight. She had a Winchester rifle leveled at us.

"Melanie!" Manny gasped. His face had blanched so much that I feared for his heart. "Why are you here?"

Melanie smiled, raising her eyebrows as if trying to think of something else to place on her marketing list, then sighed wistfully. "You always were a meddling man, Manny. Guess that comes from bein' a lawyer and all, always diggin' into the private affairs of other folks."

I was tongue-tied with the rifle pointed at us, and the shock of Melanie's confrontation. My mind raced to put facts into feasible sequence, to find any clue to why Melanie would have tracked us to Juan's house. My blood turned to ice water as the jumbled realization, the incontrovertible truth, came to a skidding halt as it burst through my consciousness. Much as I didn't want to believe it, it was unavoidably, glaringly obvious.

"Now, Melanie," Manny soothed, some of his color returning to his heavily lined face, "just what brings you out here this time of night?" His tone was musical, as if he were amused at a childish prank, designed to fathom the facts without upsetting the prankster.

"Same thing as you," she replied simply. "'Cept I don't want that silly old diary. I just don't want anyone else to have it either."

"What's in the diary, Melanie? You know, don't you." It wasn't a question, but a quiet statement.

"Yes," she drawled. "Or at least, I think I know what it says. Doesn't matter much, really. S'long as nobody else gets to see it."

"How'd you know we were here?" Manny asked softly.

She shrugged off the question. "Alexander told me after you two had talked. Wasn't very smart of you to tell him what you were up to," she explained lightly. "Alex was never one to keep his mouth shut if he could seem more important by keeping it goin'."

"Does he know you're here?"

"Land sakes, of course not! Both the boys think I'm in my room and sound asleep. Told 'em I wasn't feeling too sprightly and thought I'd turn in early. And you know how protective the boys have always been about me."

Melanie waved the gun toward the couch, and we woodenly sat down awaiting her next move. I finally found my voice. "Why don't you want us to learn who killed my father?" I asked, but in my heart I already knew the answer.

"'Cause it's nobody's business!" she answered with more vehemence than I had ever thought her capable of having. "It's over. Past. More'n thirty years have gone by . . . what difference could it make now?"

"Justice, Melanie," Manny replied kindly. "That, and regaining monies long overdue to Alyce and to you and the boys."

"Fiddlesticks! We don't need any money! We've got the ranch, Pa's mine . . . the only person who ever cared about losin' out was Alexander. He's always fancied himself some sort of land baron."

"What about me, Melanie?" I posed the question more out of academic interest than genuine, and also to try to stall her until we could find a way to get the rifle away from her.

"You?" Melanie blinked her round blue eyes at me as if I'd asked an utterly stupid question.

"Yes. My share of the mine," I plied.

"Why, child, you've got us now. Kin who care about you. You'll stay on with us for as long as you wish—or marry Kyle and settle down right here in Frazier. What on earth do you want with money? Money's evil, you know." She frowned, her straight brows knitting with her thoughts. "It was greed that killed Mitchell, goin' off in search of that gold mine. Money's bad, Alyce."

I stole a glance at Manny to see if I could discern his thoughts, but his stoic expression told me that he was not going to risk betraying his thoughts while Melanie held us at rifle point.

"Mitchell died," he began gently, "because he found himself in a fight with a mountain lion—and he lost. It could've happened at any time, and to anyone who goes hunting. Melanie," he added, "searchin' for the gold had nothing to do with his death."

Melanie stiffly nodded her head in stubborn insistence. "Yes it did, Manny. And it was her pa that got him all worked up about it!"

"Are you saying that my father forced a grown man to go on some wild-goose chase?"

"Now, that would've happened anyway and you know it," Manny said slowly, calmly. "Your own father had searched for the Lost Mine of the Padres."

"And it killed him, too!"

"Many men have come to unexpected death while searching for it," he interrupted. "It doesn't mean that the mine itself killed them, and you know it. Every one of them died from quite ordinary causes—exposure, rattlers, falling from a horse and breaking their damn-fool necks. . . ."

"It was the lust for gold that did it," she acknowledged grudgingly.

A sudden silence fell between us and I watched Melanie's warm, friendly face wrestle with the information—that, or from some inner confusion befuddling her. The ticking of a clock somewhere sounded like a hammer as we quietly watched Melanie's eyes cloud with her thoughts. It was awful. I ached to comfort her, to put my arms about her and tell her everything would be all right—but I couldn't. The barrel of the Winchester held me captive on the couch.

Her head tilted in jerking motions as her mind struggled through the maze of her own private hell, but she never took her eyes from us, nor lowered the rifle. Her mouth was working strangely, and I feared that she might pull the trigger mistakenly as her torment writhed within her head. At long last, Manny tried to get through to her, to bring her back to the present. "Melanie," he said, his voice as soft as a breeze, "why are you trying to protect Juan?"

As soon as the words were out, the front door burst open as

if kicked. Juan charged through the room, but not before Melanie spun in his direction and fired at him.

In a flurry, even before Juan had hit the floor, gripping his shoulder with blood oozing through his fingers, Manny moved with an alacrity that belied his years, and wrenched the rifle away from Melanie's grasp. She stared at him for a few moments, then turned to me. Her eyes seemed glazed, and a light smile played across her lips. "I'm sorry," she said in a little girl's voice, her head moving from side to side. "I'm sorry," she repeated.

Manny gently drew her to the divan, and I moved to help Juan. He had managed to sit up, but his blood had left a jagged circle on the rug—an ugly testament to our intrusion. *If it jeopardizes someone enough to kill for his secret* echoed over and over in my ears.

✻☙✻

Juan's shoulder was bandaged by Doc Adams. The dawn came up at El Fin del Camino but promised no surcease from the grim and shattering events of the previous night. Manny had driven over to Kyle's house and had brought him back; I'd driven Juan to the ranch house for what we all had to face, to acknowledge. Although none of us really expected that Melanie would cause any more damage, just to be sure, we secured her in a crude, but effective way: Using two of Juan's jackets, we placed her arms in one, backward, like a strait jacket; then wrapped the other facing forward and buttoned it all the way down. She smiled the entire time and offered no resistance whatsoever. We put her between us in Juan's car, and I drove us to the house in humble silence, tears of empathy and remorse spilling down my cheeks. There was nothing I could say that would undo what had happened. Juan had been right; I had been wrong. Shuddering with my guilt, I didn't trust my voice to utter a word.

Once back at the house, I roused Alexander and William; and Juan and I waited in the living room while they donned robes to join us. Juan asked for a drink, and I got him one submissively, silently. I felt a stupid, insolent fool. As I placed the glass on the table before him, his good hand reached into his coat pocket and pulled out a book with no title: Carlos Melendez's diary.

He placed it next to the glass, not even looking at me. No scathing accusations; no withering glances. Juan just took it out and put it down. It could've been yesterday's copy of *The Mountain Enterprise:* mundane, useless, and not worthy of discussion—instead of what it really was. Because of that rather small book, Mary Gomez was dead; Kyle could have died; Juan had been injured; and poor, lovable Melanie was quite insanely in another world.

"Ever since Kyle revealed its existence," Juan began softly, "I've kept it with me. Either on my person, or in the car."

His voice was even, as if he were commenting about finding dust on his shoes. It didn't require a reply from me, even if in my heartsick state I could have made one.

Moments later, we heard William and Alexander coming down the stairs and I watched them enter the room feeling sick to my stomach with the burden of my responsibility. William was the first to notice Melanie seated in her favorite chair, trussed in her two jackets. He crossed over to her, bent down, then looked into her eyes for a long moment. When he straightened up, his eyes were brimmed with tears.

"What's this all about!" Alexander demanded sharply, his shoulders back and his chin held high.

I couldn't reply. Quicksand had swallowed my energies, and sealed me into the morass of my culpability.

Juan took a brief swallow from his drink, then placed the glass on the table next to the diary. He rubbed his eyes wearily. "It's a long story, Alex," he said slowly.

Ben came shuffling into the room just as the sounds of the four-wheeler coming to a halt outside reached us. Manny opened the door and helped Kyle over to a chair, then moved to the fireplace and began to stoke up the embers.

"Will someone have the decency to tell me what's happened!" Alex shouted, his control obviously only barely contained.

It was more than I could bear. I sank to the sofa, weeping softly, not caring who could see my remorse. Ben made a move toward me, but Alex put a restraining hand on his shoulder. I didn't care. All that had happened was because of me; it was only right that I should suffer without pity or sympathy.

Juan tapped the diary. "It's all here, in essence," he said.

"How long have you been in possession of the journal?" Kyle asked in a flat voice.

"Years. I found it one day when my father asked me to bring him something from his desk. I opened the wrong drawer, and there it was."

"And you read it," Kyle prompted.

"Not right then, but later—when my father wasn't home."

Manny went to the sideboard and fixed himself a drink without consent. "I still don't understand," he said as he turned toward us, glancing only briefly at Melanie's happy, smiling face, "why it is Melanie felt she had to protect you or your father."

Juan sighed, wincing at the pain in his shoulder. "She wasn't," he said after a moment.

"Then . . ." Manny said.

"She was protecting herself," Juan said.

"Let me see that journal!" Kyle's face showed total disbelief.

"It's all here," Juan said, handing the innocent-looking book to Manny to pass along. "Melanie murdered Horatio Laird. She was only seventeen, but she killed him."

Manny stepped over and gripped my shoulder in solace. It was kind of him, but I was beyond anyone's support. I'd recognized the truth when Melanie's voice reached us in Juan's darkened living room. It had all fallen into place like the last stone in an avalanche. Destructive, senseless, and futile—yet, there it was.

I had finally stopped crying, and merely sat limply, letting Juan unfold the truth for the others. "According to my father . . ."

Kyle was leafing through the entries as Juan spoke, confirming his veracity. "You discussed it with your father before he died?"

Juan nodded. "Yes. Once I'd read it, I couldn't keep silent. Not with my father, anyway. We agreed never to reveal its contents to anyone."

"Go on," Alexander said stiffly, while William gently undid the buttons of the coat about Melanie's shoulders.

"My father knew nothing about psychology," Juan began again, "but he told me that Melanie was obsessed by cloying devotion to Mitchell. That she'd only loved two people in her entire life—fanatically so, that is. One was her mother, whom she lost to Horatio Laird; at least, in her mind she did. Then, when Horatio encouraged Mitchell to search for the gold mine, spent long hours talking about the old fables and myths —and as a result, he ended up dead . . ."

"Her mind snapped," Manny finished for him.

"Not totally," Juan said. "She'd simply block out anything she didn't want to think about. She felt quite justified in what she'd done. Horatio Laird had robbed her of her two most beloved people, and she merely acted out an eye-for-an-eye vengeance. But none of us knew what was in her head, how capable of rational thinking she might be. While Melanie was able to dart in and out, at least surfacely, we thought she'd become psychotic enough to obliterate the memory of her deed—that she was, at that point, quite harmless. Obviously, we were wrong."

"Are you saying that Melanie didn't love us, her own brothers?" Alex blustered.

Juan waved his hand in negation. "Of course not. What I'm saying is that there were only two people for whom Melanie had an irrational, psychotic, possessive love."

"Then who threatened our mother till she had to leave Frazier? Not Melanie! Not if she was so possessive of her mother, and at that point had her all to herself!" Alex reasoned hotly.

"No, it wasn't she. My father did."

Heads came around smartly at that remark, even mine. "But *why?*" I asked, totally surprised by the information.

"I can see why," Kyle said slowly. "Because you'd been born. You were her next rival. You'd be next."

Juan's eyes closed in agreement. "It was just common sense, the next logical move in an illogical mentality. It would've broken your mother's heart to learn that her own daughter had killed Horatio, and, of course, to bring it out in the open would have necessitated legal prosecution."

There was a brief quiet while all of us tried to assimilate this shocking information. Only Juan and his father had known Melanie's guilty secret all those years, keeping it from the rest of the world in the belief that Melanie had become somewhat deranged but probably harmless—provided I was removed from the scene.

"But if that's the case," Manny said, "then why did she seem so glad to see Alyce?"

"She was," Juan answered simply. "But that had nothing to do with the revelation that there was a diary that contained the truth! Alyce, as an adult and looking so much like their mother, posed no immediate real threat. Not until Kyle revealed that a diary existed. . . ."

"Then the tarantula in Melanie's room," Alex said, his whole being sagging as the truth sunk in.

"Was a genuine accident," Juan answered. "It got into the house somehow, as they frequently do in this area."

"And Mary Gomez's death?" William asked in a droning, heartsick voice.

"Was intended for effect, a threat. Or, at least, I can only surmise that. It was before she knew about the diary, but you were all so intent upon finding out who murdered Horatio Laird that you set Melanie up. She was feeling threatened, her secure niche in the world could be shattered if the truth were found out. I don't think she meant for anyone to die at that point, just to scare Alyce back to Boston."

Ben spoke up for the first time. "It was one of my rattlers," he admitted softly.

"Then why didn't you say so at the time?" William asked.

Stuffing his hands into his robe pockets, Ben replied, "Because, following the incident with the spider, I knew you'd think I was trying to kill Alyce. I didn't want to spend the rest of my life on the funny farm just because one of my snakes killed Mary!" His tone was defensive, defiant.

"Oh, Ben," Alex mumbled to himself.

"You would've blamed me and you know it! You have always treated me like an incompetent anyhow!"

Manny shook his head incredulously. "Then it was Melanie who fired at you over at Morro Flats."

"And put the poison in my scotch," Kyle added somberly.

"But why!" Alexander asked wearily. He seemed to have aged terribly during those last moments before the sun came up.

"Ask her," Juan answered, his voice on the verge of breaking.

We all looked at Melanie then, knowing that she would probably never come back to the present; never be able to answer the many questions about her deranged motives. She made a heartbreaking picture, sitting there so quietly, so gently and completely in her own world. Her sparkling blue eyes surveying the vast regions of her imaginary domain.

"I think you caught her by surprise at my house," Juan resumed, his deep voice hushed in weary sorrow. "If I'm right, she was there searching for the journal. She already knew it wasn't at Kyle's, so she'd come to search at my place."

"No," Manny said. "She knew we were on our way over to your place. And why."

"Then I have to assume she meant to kill you," Juan added, his voice trailing off.

No one said anything, and I forced myself to look from face to face. Melanie may have been a murderess, but from the expressions around me, I knew I was just as guilty as she. I rose, unsteadily, and went to my room. I'd ruined enough lives. It was time to pack and go before I ruined more. What a mess I'd made of things, what havoc I had wreaked in my search for the truth!

I left them, left all of them, unable to say a word.

CHAPTER EIGHTEEN

With tears brimming in my eyes, I pulled out my luggage and hastily began packing, mindless of tidiness or logic. I felt numb with self-reproach, an icy cold around my heart as if to ward off the warmth of life and reality. I pulled open drawers and emptied them ruthlessly into the yawning suitcases, my movements stiff and surreal in my frenzied state.

"May I come in?"

The sound of a voice pulled me up abruptly, and I whirled to see Kyle leaning against the doorjamb. I stared at him for a second, then, nodding, slumped down on the bed next to the open baggage. I was terribly close to losing control of myself, and forced myself to take a long, deep breath.

Kyle took the chair facing me, leaning forward with his forearms resting on his knees, his big hands dangling listlessly. He glanced up at me with a strange, withdrawn expression, then smiled wistfully. "You are taking this a lot harder than you need to, you know."

Almost in reflex action, I cocked my head in disbelief. "I what?"

"Look, Alyce, what's happened is not your doing any more than it's mine. All either of us wanted was to get at the truth. Well, we got it."

"And that's it?" I asked incredulously. "No sense of responsibility? No sympathy for Alexander or William? No compassion for Melanie?" I stared at Kyle as if I'd never seen him before.

He shrugged. "Let's not get all carried away," he said

slowly. "Look at the other side of it. . . . Melanie committed murder and will get away with it. How bad is that?"

"How bad!"

"Well? She isn't going to be electrocuted, or spend the rest of her life in jail. Why are you taking this so personally?"

"Kyle," I said, pausing to pull my thoughts together, trying to understand what he was saying. "Melanie isn't a cold-blooded killer, some ruthless thug getting cheap thrills at someone else's expense. She's mentally unbalanced. We're not talking about a character in a movie, but about a real woman, a warm and loving human being—unable to control her emotions, her actions." Where it came from, I wasn't sure, but I could feel my anger mounting, my face becoming flushed with the surge of inner fury.

"I could use a drink," Kyle muttered, dropping his gaze from mine.

I sighed, the trigger of my emotions uncocking and returning to its usual safety catch. Of course. Kyle wanted a drink. He was, in truth, not that different from Melanie; his avenue of escape was different but that was all. "There's some sherry in the kitchen," I said after a moment.

Kyle rose to his feet slowly, then placed his hands on my shoulders. "You think I'm weak, don't you," he said softly.

"No, Kyle. You can't get out of it that way. It's not what *I* think, it's what *you* think. It's easier to believe yourself unable to cope with life than it is to make the effort."

"Is that why you're running away?" he asked.

Involuntarily, I shook my head slowly. "I'm not running away . . . I'm going home, where I came from. I've already caused too much damage here. It's not my home, it never was. I made a terrible mistake. But I hope I've learned my lesson and I'll try to live with it." I turned then, not wanting to see the self-pitying expression on Kyle's face.

"You could stay here," he began almost inaudibly. "If you married me, it would become your home."

My mind searched for a diplomatic way to reject him, but found none. At last, I could only voice the truth. "You don't want to marry me, Kyle, you want to contract for my strength. If I married you, you'd be living with an object lesson— someone to sober up for, someone to watch over you. That's not marriage. It's prisoner and warden. If you want to straighten out your life, make something of yourself, you'll have to do it from within—not with me as a crutch. Neither of us could ever be happy with that kind of role-playing."

He leaned forward, kissed me lightly on the cheek, and then smiled boyishly. "I've a terrible feeling you're right," he said.

I was relieved at his reaction, and surprised by my own observations of the situation. At least I wouldn't be responsible for tampering with yet another person's life; perhaps I had learned my lesson better than I'd realized.

"It's in the kitchen, you said?"

I nodded wearily and watched Kyle as he slowly walked toward the door. Fervently, I hoped he'd be able to resist his impulse, but knew there was nothing I could do about it.

He turned in the hallway and grinned. "Maybe I'll just stare at the bottle for a while. We all like to have choices."

Then he was gone. I was alone in my room. No, not "my" room, but the guestroom at the Musser ranch. I had been only a guest here. Oh Mother, I thought leadenly, why did you ever leave me that letter?

Ben drove me to the airport in Bakersfield around midday. "It's not your fault, you know," he said as we pulled up to the terminal.

I tried to smile, but failed. "Thank you, Ben. I don't know if I'll ever believe it, but I'm glad you don't think I'm to blame."

As I placed my hand on the door handle, Ben leaned over and kissed me lightly on the cheek. "It's I who should thank you," he said.

"What do you mean?"

"You cared about me, about my future. I've given a lot of thought to our talk."

I was too dumfounded to comment, but I was pleased that I'd not destroyed everyone at El Fin del Camino. "I'm going away," Ben added. "I'm going to move to San Francisco and see if I can begin to live my own life. I'd like it," he said almost shyly, "if we could stay in touch . . . if I could write to you occasionally."

Somehow, knowing that Ben didn't hold the events my

presence had brought about against me comforted me enormously. Perhaps there was hope that everyone in Frazier could someday forgive me. . . . Relieved tears stung my eyes. "I should like that very much," I said, and scrambled out of the car before my emotions ran away from me.

Ben climbed out and handed my luggage to the waiting porter. He gave me a swift hug, then got back into the car and drove away.

It was with very mixed feelings that I followed the skycap toward the check-in counter, my eyes misted with unresolved conflict and a sense of great loss. Would I ever see my brothers again? Could they ever forgive me? And I didn't dare contemplate what Kyle and Juan thought of me. No wonder Juan had been so adamant about sending me packing! He'd known the truth all along; knew that the only way to preserve it, and to stop Melanie from harming anyone else, was to get me away from there—to remove the threat named Alyce Prather Laird. And I thought of Melanie as I last saw her, flanked by Alexander and William as they drove off to the sanitarium.

Oh, they'd both said I wasn't responsible, both men hugging me and saying their farewells as best they could under the circumstances. But I couldn't believe that they were sincere; they were only being polite to a relative who was, at long overdue last, going back to where she came from. It would be a long time before they'd be able to look at me and not associate the anguish I had evoked with my face.

With dragging, heavy steps, I reached the airline counter and managed to drag out that I wanted to go to Boston, connecting out of wherever was necessary. Boston. Home. Away from all the awful things for which I'd been responsible.

"You can connect out of Los Angeles or San Francisco, miss," the girl said. "Any preference?"

"No," I said sincerely. "It makes no difference at all." I opened my handbag to remove the traveler's checks, and a strong, tanned hand closed over mine.

"Where I come from, the gentleman picks up the tab," he said.

I whirled, joy rising in my throat. Juan put his arms around   G 50 me tightly, clasping me to his strong chest. "You'll not mind if I come along? I've never been to Boston."

"Oh Juan! Juan! I thought . . ."

He grinned down at me. "Even if I'd been able to convince you to return to Boston earlier . . . I'd have followed you there. If . . . if you wouldn't mind a civil ceremony, San Francisco's a beautiful place for a honeymoon."

"My beautiful, too-serious darling," I began. But I could say no more, and happy tears ran freely down my face as Juan's mouth closed over mine. This old maid was wildly, crazily in love with the most wonderful man in the world.

.